The Best Friend Problem

The Best Friend Problem

Mariah Ankenman

Entangled Publishing, LLC
2614 South Timberline Road
Suite 105, PMB 159
Fort Collins, CO 80525
rights@entangledpublishing.com

Lovestruck is an imprint of Entangled Publishing, LLC.

Edited by Stacy Abrams and Judi Lauren
Cover design by Bree Archer
Cover photography by Lumina/Stocksy
FollowTheFlow/GettyImages

Manufactured in the United States of America

First Edition August 2019

To all the first responders who put their life on the line in the service and care of others.
Thank you.

Chapter One

Men sucked. And Prudence Carlson didn't mean that metaphorically.

Her last date had literally sucked her finger into his mouth five minutes after they met. She supposed he was trying to be sensual, licking the bit of whipped cream she'd scooped up from her hot cocoa, but it had just creeped. Her. Out.

And left her with no whipped cream.

He'd been the latest disappointment in a long line of horrible dates. Which was why she'd deleted all her dating apps and sworn off men for good.

After a string ot shallow high school relationships—the best of which lasted all of six months—dozens of bad first dates, and Terrence the Terrible, her ex who was supposed to be The One but after two years together, left her the second he got a shiny job offer halfway across the country…she was done.

Admittedly, that wasn't entirely fair of her. Terrence had offered her the chance to move with him, but at the time, she'd been starting up her own business with her friends. A move wasn't in the plan, and long distance hadn't appealed to either of them.

I can't pass up this opportunity, Pru.

But he *could* pass up on her. On their future.

Whatever. She was over it. Over him.

Now, anyway.

It had taken almost eight months and an entire store's worth of rocky road ice cream to navigate that rocky road of abandonment. But when she'd jumped back into the dating game, her heart just hadn't had any trust in romance.

Even her parents, rest their souls, most days had been so wrapped up in each other, they'd completely forgotten they had a daughter.

Pru tugged on her ponytail, adjusting the perfect hairstyle. There was no sense in focusing on the past. Paying the "what if" game only led to heartbreak. If Pru wanted to achieve her goals, she had to think about the future, her heart's desire.

Too bad she needed a guy to get her heart's desire.

"No," she spoke to herself in her empty bedroom. "I don't need a guy. I just need his…stuff."

Glancing at the binder in her lap, she turned the page she'd been staring at for the past ten minutes, jotting down her notes in the yellow notepad at her side. Page after page of pictures, facts, bios, and health histories filled her brain, each one going onto the pros and cons checklist she was compiling so she could select the perfect candidate. The perfect donor.

The perfect second set of DNA for my baby.

Ever since she'd received her first baby doll at seven, Pru knew she wanted to be a mother, to have a family. One like the families she saw on TV. They always looked so happy and loving. Logically, she knew they were all actors playing roles and that family problems didn't get solved in half an hour with a laugh track behind you. Still, art imitated life, right? It had to exist.

And since she'd never had anything like that, she'd create one herself.

A family.

Something she lost too young. The void in her heart, the aching, yawning hole, had gotten smaller over the years, filled by her loving great-aunt and wonderful friends, but it hadn't disappeared completely. She didn't think it ever would, but she knew creating her own family would help. Start something new—wasn't that what life was all about?

At one time, she thought she could start that family with Terrence, but...

Whatever. That ship sailed long ago. He hadn't been The One like she'd thought.

The One is just a silly fairy tale used to sell movies and merchandise.

Great Aunt Rose's oft-spoken words rang loudly in her head, as if the woman were sitting right beside her on the creaky ten-year-old mattress instead of resting peacefully in Fairmount Cemetery. A sharp pang struck her chest, dead center.

"Miss you, Auntie Rose."

The silent room didn't answer, but she didn't expect it to. Pru didn't believe in anything as silly as ghosts. Her best friend, Finn, had given her the nickname Practical Pru, and she supposed it fit. Better than wishing on stars and hoping your dreams came true. If you wanted something, you had to work hard and make it happen.

"And that is exactly what I'm doing." She glanced at the new information on the page she'd just turned. "With the help of one of you generous gentlemen, of course."

The whole traditional way to get a family hadn't been working for her. And who said a family had to look like *Even Stevens*? Families came in all shapes and sizes. So she couldn't find or trust a man to stay by her side through thick and thin. So what? If she wanted a baby, there were advances in science and guys willing to fill a cup for fifty bucks.

Thanks to them, Pru could take destiny into her own hands.

An image of a tiny, squishy, squirming baby filled her mind. Moisture gathered in her eyes, and she sniffed as a wave of longing washed over her. Her arms ached to hold her future baby. To shower the little peanut with all the love she had. When she pressed a hand to her chest, the strong beat of her heart pounded against her palm, every thump hitting with a steady surge that seemed to echo one word in her mind...

Baby, baby, baby.

For the past five years, she'd scrimped and saved, even with the ups and downs of starting a wedding planning business with her roommates—yes, she saw the irony in a woman who planned happily-ever-afters for a living not believing in them herself—and she'd managed to stash away a nice nest egg for the fertility treatments and upcoming baby expenses.

Pru was nothing if not a planner and expert budgeter. That's why she handled the books for Mile High Happiness, the wedding planning company she and her two roommates ran. Denver had been experiencing a boom lately thanks to all Colorado had to offer: the majestic mountain peaks, the bustling city, and the legal...plant life.

Starting a business was always a risk, but the picturesque appeal of the Mile High City and surrounding areas made it a premier wedding destination for locals and visitors alike. Six years in and the women were successfully running in the black with no signs of slowing down. She had her awesome friends, an amazing job, and a padded savings account. Now all Pru needed was her baby.

"So, who's the lucky fella going to be?"

A loud chime made her jump before she realized it

wasn't the book of donors answering her but her cell phone indicating a text message. She snorted, silently chiding herself for her silliness, reaching for her phone.

F: *Need a rescue.*

The best friend code.

She and Finn had made a pact in high school: if either of them was on a bad date and needed rescuing, the other would drop everything and come right away. Though she'd been on numerous bad dates with creeps, jerks, and just plain bores, she'd only used their code a handful of times. She preferred to end things herself. Finn, however, despite his muscular physique and plethora of tattoos, was a big ol' softie and could never end a date without an excuse—no matter how badly it was going.

If she had a dollar for every time he'd used the code, she could have paid for ten babies by now.

P: *Where?*

F: *Strikers*

Oh, goody, the dimly lit pool hall that still reeked of cigarettes even though smoking indoors had been banned in Colorado since before she'd been legally allowed in bars. She sighed. Time to put on her BFF pants and rescue her sweet but clueless bestie.

The man really needed to learn how to end a date that wasn't going well. Maybe she should give him a cheat sheet of easy-out excuses.

Although, truthfully, she didn't mind that her friend needed her.

Taking care of the people in her life gave Pru a sense of warmth deep in her heart. When her friends were happy, she was happy. So she didn't mind rescuing Finn from bad dates or making sure her roommate, Mo, drank enough water after a midnight margarita party, or even seeing to the needs of her great aunt during her last years, as the old woman's health had failed her.

Closing her binder, she tucked it and the notepad into her bedside drawer before heading out of her room.

"Going out?"

She glanced into the kitchen table as she passed, spotting her roommate and business partner, Lilly Walsh, sitting in one of the dark oak chairs they'd bought at a thrift store, a pile of seating charts spread out before her on the table.

"Yep. Best-friend rescue duty calls."

"I don't understand why that man has such trouble dating," Moira Rossi, her other roommate and business partner, said as she closed the fridge door, a slice of cake in hand. "He's a solid twelve. How does he have so many bad dates? If I went out with him, I'd have my panties off before we got to dessert."

"You have your panties off with an eight before salads, Mo," Lilly gibed without looking up from her charts.

"Yeah, but that's because I enjoy exploring my sexuality. Not all of us live the stifled life of a nineteenth-century crone."

Pru chuckled as Lilly sighed with a shake of her head. Mo simply smiled, shoving a bite of cake into her mouth. The three women were as different as night and day, but they'd all been assigned as roommates in college, and somehow, they'd just clicked and been together ever since.

"Honestly, Pru," Mo continued, sitting at the table and offering Lilly a forkful of cake. Predictably, the dark-haired woman waved her off, preferring salty snacks over sweet ones. "I do not know how you're friends with Finn and don't demand benefits. I bet he gives really, *really* good benefits."

First of all, ew.

Second of all, she and Finn had been friends since the

seventh grade.

Sure, she wasn't stupid. She knew her bestie was what some might call insanely hot. His deep blue eyes and sandy blond hair gave him the perfect boy-next-door look. His full tattooed sleeves and the undercut hairstyle he sported gave him a bad-boy vibe. The man was what Aunt Rose had referred to as a walking hot flash. Then there was his job. As a firefighter, Finn was a bona fide hero. What woman could resist that?

Me.

Yes, her bestie was hot, and a hero, but they'd been friends too long for her to throw everything away for one night of sex. And it *would* be one night. Much like he'd given her a nickname, she'd given him one: First Date Finn. Because the women who did make it to a first date rarely saw a second.

Finn liked to keep it light and fun. And no way would Pru risk their years of solid friendship just for *fun*. She'd lost too much in her life. She refused to lose Finn, too.

"I'm leaving before you make me vomit."

She grabbed her jacket and headed out the apartment door to the sound of Mo laughing. The elevator was notorious for taking forever, so Pru skipped it and made her way down the stairs. She needed the cardio anyway. A healthy body was important for the plans she had.

The sharp chill of night air smacked her in the face as she pushed open the exit door and headed outside. Being mid-October, the days were still pretty warm, but the city cooled at night. Not cold enough to warrant hopping in her car, though—the bar was only a few blocks away, and parking in Denver was a bitch.

It took less than ten minutes to get there. Once she showed her ID to the bouncer, she headed inside. Loud cracks and the smack of hard plastic billiard balls assaulted her ears, and the low din of conversation followed close behind. Her eyes took a moment to adjust to the dim light of the room. Strikers was located just off the 16th Street Mall, where large buildings with bright lights and businesses with flashy signs lined the street.

After a few blinks, she could see the room clearly. The bar along the far wall was packed, as always, with people clamoring for the bartender's attention. Twelve large pool tables took up the center of the room, all occupied but none of them sporting a six-foot-tall tatted firefighter desperately trying to escape a date.

She moved farther into the room, ignoring the catcalls and disgusting propositions from a table of drunk men, one of whom appeared to be a future groom, if the Last Night of Freedom T-shirt was anything to go by.

Ugh.

In her years planning weddings, she'd seen everything, from solid relationships to disasters waiting to happen. She tried to believe in love—it was a part of her job, after all— but people made it so hard sometimes. Didn't matter. She handled the *finances*. Lilly and Mo dealt with the clients, and they believed, Mo especially, in all that mushy crap enough for all of them.

At the back of the pool hall was a sparse collection of small high-top tables, where she finally spotted the object of her quest. Finn sat at one of the tables with a woman who was chatting away, vibrantly waving her hand in the air as she spoke. She didn't look like a serial killer. Light blond hair, cute black dress, spiky red shoes Pru knew Lilly would kill for. A pleasant smile lit her face as she continued speaking, barely pausing to take a breath. Pru didn't see what was so wrong with this woman that Finn needed to text her for backup.

But he had. So here she was. Duty called.

"Hey, Finn. I'm so glad I found you." She hurried over

to the table, making sure she sounded breathless, as if she'd run the five blocks from her apartment. Must have worked because Chatterbox immediately closed her mouth. "You have to come home right away."

Blondie glared at Finn, a murderous rage suddenly lighting her eyes. "Oh shit, not again!"

Huh, maybe she *was* a serial killer.

"You're married, aren't you, you bastard!"

"What?" Finn held up his hands. "No, I'm not. This is my friend Pru."

She'd say one thing for her bestie: He may not know how to break off a date well, but he sure as hell would never use a cruel lie to do it.

"Oh, sorry." Blondie winced. "I don't mean to jump to conclusions but I've had a few bad experiences with guys saying they're single when they're not."

Pru nodded. *Preaching to the choir, sister.*

"So, what's wrong?"

She glanced over at Finn. Oh right, she was supposed to be rescuing him.

Usually they used the "personal emergency" excuse. Vague, urgent, but nothing horrible. Tonight, though, Pru found herself in a mood. Finn had dragged her away from important donor research. Not that he knew that, because she hadn't shared her plan with him yet—or anyone else, for that matter. And here he was with a woman who seemed perfectly nice, if a little chatty, and he couldn't work up a single "I don't think this is working"?

Trying her best to hide her smile, she shook her head sadly. "It's Bruiser."

"Bruiser?"

"His dog," she said, answering the confused woman's question.

Finn's chair scraped loudly, threatening to tip over with

the force as he stood. "Bru Baby? What happened? Is she okay?"

She felt slightly guilty for the look of panic in her best friend's gaze. Slightly. He deserved *some* panic for being such a wuss that he needed a rescue from an easily escapable date.

"I think she got into your fungus cream again."

His eyes narrowed, catching on. "Oh, did she now?"

"Yup." She rolled her lips to keep the laughter from escaping.

"You have a dog?"

He turned to face his date, panic abated since he knew Pru was messing with him and his fur baby was fine. Finn didn't have any fungus cream in his apartment. The annoying guy didn't even have the decency to get athlete's foot and create a bit of physical disgust she could crow to Mo about.

"Yes. A rescue. Adopted her two years ago."

His date gave a sort of smile-frown. "Oh, that's sweet, but I'm allergic to dogs. And cats. All animals, really. I tried to get a hamster once, but I ended up with red eyes and a swollen throat two hours in."

"Oh. I guess this won't work out, then."

For crap's sake! She came all the way over here to rescue him, and all he had to do to get out of the date was mention his dog? Finn owed her big time.

"I guess not, but it was nice to meet you. I hope your dog is okay."

After making sure his date had a ride home—because even if he couldn't break a date, Finn never left anyone stranded—they made their way out of the bar and onto the streets.

"I can't believe you used my dog as an excuse." Finn glared at her. "We agreed never to make it personal."

"And I can't believe you still can't tell a woman 'things aren't working out' like a grown-ass man."

"Not all of us are as blunt as you, Pru. Some of us have sensitive feelings that bruise easily."

She snorted, rolling her eyes, because if there was one thing Finn didn't do, it was bruise easily, in his feelings *or* body. Her bestie was a rock.

Still, he did care about others to the point of sacrificing his own happiness at times. Finn cared too much. Probably why he became a firefighter. Finn hated seeing anyone in any kind of pain.

"Fine. I'm sorry for using Bruiser as an excuse."

He grinned, the left side of his mouth ticking up higher than the right, as it always did. Slinging an arm around her shoulders, he gave her a squeeze.

"It's all good. Thanks for bailing me out. Bailey was nice, but I couldn't get a word in edgewise with that woman. She talked nonstop from the moment we sat down until you showed up. The minute she said she likes Wes Craven movies I knew it was a bust."

"You could have just told her about the time you cowered under the blankets like a big ol' baby during *Chucky*." Pru chuckled. "That would have turned her off in a heartbeat."

He glared, nudging her with his hip as they walked. "I didn't 'cower like a baby.' I was checking my phone and didn't want the light from the screen to affect your viewing."

She snorted. "Sure, you were just being considerate."

"I was. Besides, that doll is creepy as hell." He shuddered. "Toys should not come to life, especially with the soul of a serial killer inside them."

Her bestie would run into a burning building without a thought about the danger, but that same guy was too scared to watch anything with psycho killers or ghosts. She did not get it.

"Why'd you go out with her in the first place?"

He shrugged. "We both swiped right."

Charming. Sometimes she so did not understand her generation.

"So, where'd you park?"

"Park? On a Saturday night? Are you kidding me?" She shook her head. "I walked."

The smile left his face, brow turning down with disapproval. His large, muscular arms, covered with amazing works of inked art, crossed over his chest as he stared her down. Not hard to do, since he stood a good seven inches above her.

"You walked? At this time of night?"

"Yes, *Dad*. I've lived in the city for most of my life. I know my way around."

Gaze narrowing, he bent until his nose almost touched hers. "So have I. Which is how I know it's not safe to walk the city streets alone at night. Dammit, Pru, I never would have texted if I knew you were going to walk by yourself."

She knew he was only looking out for her, but it still made her angry that he was right. Walking at night in the city wasn't the smartest move for a woman alone. Another reason why men sucked.

"Come on, I'll give you a ride back."

He started walking toward the curb where his 2011 Harley-Davidson Sportster was parked. Reaching into the side bag, he grabbed his extra helmet and tossed it to her. She caught the heavy safety equipment, shaking her head as she slipped it on.

"I still think it's stupid you bought this thing."

The used motorcycle was his pride and joy, second only to his dog.

"You can't even ride it half the year." Motorcycles and snow did not get along.

"Yeah," he said, strapping his helmet on and straddling the large bike. "But I can ride it the other half."

Solid point. But she still thought it was a silly purchase. Her pragmatic brain couldn't wrap itself around six-months of idleness for such an expensive item.

"Hop on, and I'll take you to get food before I drop you off."

"You better." She slid behind him, wrapping her arms around his waist. "You owe me an extra-large chili cheese fry and a large strawberry shake for tonight."

He chuckled, the vibrations rumbling through his back and into her chest, which was pressed up firmly against him. For safety reasons, of course.

"Extra-large chili cheese fries and a strawberry shake coming up."

"*Large* strawberry shake. Don't get cheap on me, Jamison."

Finn started the bike, the engine rumbling to life between her legs. The bike might be useless during the winter months, but it did have its advantages. If she weren't so terrified of crashing every second she rode this damn thing, she might get one herself just to rev it up and *enjoy* the ride.

"*Large* strawberry shake," he agreed on a shout, right before he backed them up and took off down the street.

Pru held tight, eyes squeezed shut as she accepted the terrifying thrill of riding something doctors so often referred to as "donor mobiles." Her night might have been interrupted, her plans for specimen selection slightly delayed, but it was okay. She was sure that when she was a mother, she'd have to learn to adjust and go with the flow. Besides, Finn had needed her, and she'd always be there for him, just like he was always there for her.

But will he be there when I become a mom?

She honestly didn't know.

She knew she needed to talk to him about all this, and her roommates, too. She wasn't the only one affected by her decision, even if she was doing it alone. As soon as she picked a donor, things would start progressing. The people in her life needed to know about her decision before that happened. They'd support her. She was sure of it.

Mostly sure.

Pretty sure.

Didn't matter. She wanted this, and she was going to do it no matter what anyone said. So yes, she'd tell Lilly and Mo and Finn. Just maybe not tonight.

Tonight was all about those delicious chili cheese fries.

Chapter Two

The blare of her cell phone's morning alarm woke Pru from a deeply restful sleep. She always slept better once she'd made an important decision. And last night, after scarfing down Bruiser's weight in chili cheese fries, she'd come to one. She had to tell her friends about her plans now. No more putting it off. She had narrowed her list of potential donors to ten, and once she made her final decision, things would move quickly.

Of course, she knew the chances of becoming pregnant on the first try were slim, five to fifteen percent, at best. But she had enough saved for four tries. Eventually, hopefully, one would stick, and it wouldn't be long before she started showing.

She had to tell Lilly and Mo first. They'd be the ones most impacted, since Pru would need to take some time off after the baby was born. Thankfully, most of her work for the business involved budgeting and collecting and distributing payments, work she could easily do with her laptop and wifi.

After she told her roommates, she'd tell Finn.

Finn.

For the first time in all their years of friendship, she was nervous to share something with her best friend. She knew he'd support her—Finn always had, even when she'd declared a major in business and accounting instead of pre-law like her great aunt had encouraged her to do. Finn had her back. Always.

So why was she scared to tell him her plans?

Maybe because it had to do with babies, and babies usually meant sex, and sex was one topic they'd silently agreed never to discuss. They might be friends and rescue each other from bad dates, but she and Finn never, ever discussed their past sexual experiences. That would just be…weird.

Tossing off the covers, she hopped out of bed, threw on some clothes, and headed out to the kitchen. The strong, rich scent of coffee hit her nostrils the moment she opened her door. Lilly must be up already.

Not a surprise. Lilly coined the term "early riser." In college, Pru and Mo never needed to set an alarm because they knew Lilly would be up and on their butts at the crack of dawn.

Sure enough, as she stepped into the kitchen, there sat Lilly, coffee in hand, paper on the tabletop in front of her. "Morning," Pru said.

"Good morning. Coffee's ready." Lilly didn't glance up from the paper she was perusing, just pushed her black-framed glasses up her nose when they slid down. Pru made her way to the pot, grabbing the cup filled with cream and sugar Lilly had already prepared for her and pouring the sweet nectar of life into it. Her roommate spoiled her, and she loved the woman for it.

"What's that?"

Lilly answered, nose still turned down, eyes focused on her paperwork. "The Mendez-Franklin wedding. They want to push up the date by two months, so we need to shift some things around. Difficult but not impossible."

"Ugh! Please don't tell me you're working already."

Pru glanced up as Mo shuffled into the kitchen. Curly blond hair streaked with bits of red and blue dye frizzed around her head in a multicolored poof, and her robe hung off her shoulders, open to reveal her sunshine and rainbow pajamas.

"We have an emergency," Lilly answered, still focused on the work before her.

"We also have an office," Mo replied. "Downstairs. That we pay rent for so we don't bring our work home."

She had a point. Four years ago, Pru had managed to convince Lilly an office space was in the budget and a good idea. They couldn't bring clients to their apartment for consultations; no one would take them seriously. Luckily, an office on the first floor had become available for a reasonable price, and since they lived in the building, the owner had knocked off another hundred bucks a month. Sometimes it paid to be a new urbanite.

"Yes," Lilly agreed, "but you rarely get dressed before nine, and as I said, we have an emergency."

"Who the hell gets dressed before nine?"

Lilly finally glanced up, raising one dark brown brow and pointing to herself and Pru.

"E*t tu*, Brute?"

Pru simply shrugged and smiled at her very non-morning friend.

"I've only been up and dressed for about ten minutes if it helps."

"It does not," Mo said. "Not when arguing with the queen of punctuality."

"Get your coffee and get over here—we have things to discuss."

Mo rolled her eyes and made a gagging motion. Pru

chuckled into her coffee, crossing the tiny kitchen to sit at the table. The women shared a small three-bedroom apartment. Well, actually, it was a two bedroom with a glass-door office, which Lilly had strung curtains across and claimed as her room. No one would wake her with their morning noise, since the woman woke before the sun.

No one right now, anyway.

She supposed she would have to move out once she had the baby. She, Lilly, and Mo had roomed together since freshman year of college. They'd been through late-night cram sessions, all-night crying jags, and sock-on-the-door sleeping in the common area evenings. And of course, her sweet friends had been there with gallons of ice cream during the abandonment by Terrence the Terrible. But they'd never had to deal with a crying baby waking them up at all hours of the night, something Pru was looking forward to, in part, but that her friends hadn't signed on for.

She knew her friends would never kick her out, but what single twenty-eight-year-old woman wanted to live with a crying baby?

I do.

Her heart clenched with the inner whispered confession. But that was her choice, her decision. Not her friends'. She had to give them the opportunity to express how her decision might affect them. It wasn't like the women planned on living together forever. She knew Lilly was saving for a house and Mo, the eternal optimist, believed she'd find her one true soul mate, settle down, and live happily ever after before her thirtieth birthday.

"Hey, guys, I have something I need to tell you."

Both women immediately looked up from their tasks. Crap, had her tone sounded too doom and gloom? This was meant to be happy news, but the thought of leaving her friends struck a melancholy chord.

"Oh my God, you're dying!"

Mo, ever the dramatic one.

Pru rolled her eyes. "No, I'm not dying. This is good news. Or it will be, but it will change some things."

Mo hurried to the table, coffee in hand, and sat next to Lilly, who watched Pru with focused interest. Pru took the seat by Mo, facing Lilly, and glanced back and forth between her friends. Nerves fluttered in her stomach like a swarm of angry bees. Better to just put it out there, like ripping off a bandage. Let it go and hope for the best.

"I'm going to have a baby."

Two jaws flopped open, green and brown eyes going wide as her friends stared at her.

"You're pregnant!" Mo's excited scream nearly burst her eardrum.

"You shouldn't be drinking coffee in your condition."

Lilly reached for her mug, but Pru pulled it back. No one deprived her of caffeine.

Besides, she'd gotten assurance from her OB-GYN that a cup a day was perfectly safe during pregnancy.

"I'm not pregnant. Yet."

Mo scrunched her nose, the tiny freckles crossing the bridge folding together. "What do you mean, yet?"

"I've decided to go it alone and use a donor. IUI." At her friends' confused looks, she explained, "Intrauterine Insemination. And if that fails, I'll move on to In Vitro Fertilization."

At their continued silence and baffled looks, Pru pressed on.

"You both know I've always wanted to be a mom. And while I'm sure there are a lot of nice men out there, I'm just not sure there's one out there for me—"

"Don't say that, Pru." Mo held a hand to her heart, a stricken expression scrunching her brow. "Everyone has a soul mate. You'll find yours; you just need to keep looking."

She'd *been* looking. For years. At one point she'd thought she found him, but then he'd found something else. Something more important than her. Terrence hadn't even informed her he was looking for work out of state. What did that say about their relationship?

She'd misjudged him, misjudged their relationship. And yeah, maybe she'd been a little reluctant to trust since then. A little wary of what guys said versus what they actually did. Could anyone blame her?

She was tired of looking. Tired of relying on someone else to fulfill her dream. Though women were having babies later and later in life, she knew the older she got, the harder it would be. For her, especially, according to her doctor and the results of her fertility test. Maybe she would meet her one and only someday—she wasn't going to hold her breath—but she didn't want to hold out for that slim hope and miss her chance of becoming a mom.

A piece of her was missing. She had an emptiness inside, a part of her identity not yet realized. One that could only come to light when she held her soft, sweet child in her arms, raised them with all the love she had in her soul, kissed their boo-boos and wiped their tears away.

She wanted a baby more than she wanted a man.

"I'm not hanging my dreams on a possibility," she answered honestly, a heavy weight in her chest at the thought of all the years of hoping to find her prince charming only to face frog after frog.

"There're plenty of fish in the sea."

Raising her mug, she skewered Mo with what Finn called her bullshit glare. "There's also a lot of garbage."

Lilly snorted into her coffee mug. "Amen to that."

"I promise this won't affect the business," she told them. "Obviously, I will have to take a little time off when the baby is born, but I can still manage my full workload and be a mom."

"Well, of course you can." Lilly set her mug down with a sharp smack. "Women can be CEOs and single mothers. We've been raising babies on our own since the dawn of time. I have every confidence in your ability to manage a work-life balance."

"Yeah." Mo scooted her chair around, slinging her arm over Pru's shoulders. "There was a reason we called you 'mother hen' in college. You already take care of us all the time. Fixing us soup when we're sick, watching sappy rom-coms with me after a breakup even though I know they're not your fave. You're going to be the best mommy ever! Who needs a man?"

"Aren't you Team True Love?"

Her roommate shrugged. "Who says your true love has to be a romantic partner? Why can't it be your baby? Or your two awesome best buddies?"

Moisture gathered in her eyes, but she blinked back the tears. She had known her friends would be supportive, but she hadn't expected to get this emotional over their enthusiasm. Too bad she couldn't blame it on pregnancy hormones yet.

"Thanks, you guys. And I promise to start looking for a new place right away. Hopefully, I can find something before the baby gets here. Y'know, once I actually get pregnant and all."

"What?"

At Mo's stricken expression, she explained, "I'm sure you don't want to be living with a baby who wakes you up all hours of the night screaming and crying."

"And I'm sure you don't know what I want, Prudence Carlson." Removing the arm from around Pru's shoulders, Mo crossed her arms over her chest. "I happen to love babies, and I'm a very heavy sleeper."

She snuck a glance at Lilly. The polished woman, hair coiled in a perfect bun, clothes ironed with nary a wrinkle in sight, wearing three-inch heels at their kitchen table before nine in the morning, took a small sip of her coffee before adding her thoughts.

"It would be better if we moved you into my room, as the office is bigger. We might need to get a better curtain for the doors. Something thicker and more insulated. The sheer ones I have don't hold heat very well, and I've read that babies need to be kept warm. Plus, if you two are in the front of the apartment, any noise shouldn't bother us too much."

Pru's chair scraped on the hardwood floor as she rose slightly, slinging one arm around Mo and leaning over to embrace Lilly in a heartfelt hug.

"You two are seriously the best friends a girl could ask for. I love you both."

"We are pretty awesome," Mo agreed.

"And we love you, too, Pru." Lilly pulled from the hug, not as comfortable with shows of affection. "You're going to make a wonderful mother."

Standing between the two women whose opinions she valued most in this world, her eyes glossed over again. "You really think so?"

"Without a doubt."

Mo raised her coffee mug. "Of course you'll be awesome. Who was the one, senior year, who made sure I drank a gallon of water after downing two Long Island Iced Teas and a Three Kings shot?"

Spring break senior year in Las Vegas. Oooooh, she had bad memories of that trip.

Mostly of the nasty shrimp in the hotel buffet, which had her stuck in the bathroom for a day and a half. Also, of her lovable but crazy roommate's inability to turn down a dare.

"You really shouldn't have bet with those guys from Fort

Lauderdale."

"Hey, I won, didn't I?"

Yes, but she'd almost gotten alcohol poisoning in the process.

"Stupid frat boys didn't know they were messing with a high elevation chick. We are not cheap drunks."

"So, what does the IUI process entail?" Lilly asked, bringing the conversation back to the matter at hand.

Pru sat down and explained the visits to her doctor, the process of getting approval, the fertility medication the doctor had put her on, and the next steps.

"But first, I have to pick a donor."

Mo rose from her seat, heading toward the coffee pot for her second cup. "A donor?"

"Sperm donor." Pru waved her off when her friend offered the pot, while Lilly accepted. "I have a binder the office gave me with potentials. They've all been tested and cleared. And their profiles included background health, education, pictures—"

"Pictures?" Mo's lips lifted in an eager smile.

"Not the kind you're thinking of."

Her friend's smile fell. "Damn. That's no fun."

She chuckled. Leave it to Mo to think a doctor's office would offer dick pics.

"I've got it narrowed down to ten, and once I make my final pick, the doctor will set up an appointment for insemination based around my ovulation."

"Sounds practical." Lilly nodded.

"Sounds boring," Mo argued. "Babies are cool and all, but half the fun is making them. If you ask me, you're missing the good stuff, Pru."

"She wasn't asking you." Lilly pointed a finger. "She was informing us of her very well thought out and carefully planned decision. And we support her fully."

"Of course we do. To Pru, the best future mommy ever!"

Mo raised her mug; Lilly followed suit. Emotions clogged her throat, but Pru managed to raise hers as well.

"To adding another member to the Terrific Trio."

Guess they'd have to go by "Fantastic Foursome" if everything worked out as planned. Oh, she hoped everything worked out. She had a job she loved, amazingly supportive friends, and she was beginning her journey to motherhood. It might be slightly unconventional, but it was her plan, and she liked it.

Who needed a man when you had such wonderful friends at your side?

Chapter Three

"Ward, I swear to God if you don't get your ass over here and clean your dishes, I am going to shave your eyebrows in the middle of the night again!"

Finn laughed, reaching across the table to grab a card from the stack in the middle. While firefighting could be an intense, heart-pounding job when they were on a call, most of their time was spent doing rig checks, working out, and sitting around waiting for a call. Basically, he got to hang out with his friends all day. Pretty sweet job if you asked him.

Since their schedule at Denver Fire consisted of twenty-four hours on and forty-eight off, they tended to bond more than normal coworkers. That's what happened when you spent half your time living with people and responding to calls, some of them heartbreaking. To Finn, his fellow firefighters were closer than friends. They were his second family. And like all families, they loved to give each other shit.

"You better do what she says, dude. Díaz *will* do it."

Ward scowled, reaching for another card after Finn

discarded. "I know. I remember the painful four months it took to grow my damn brows back the last time. My little sister tried to teach me to draw them on, but they always looked like dying caterpillars on my forehead."

"You did look pretty ridiculous," Turner agreed, grabbing a card from the deck.

The slight curve of his fellow firefighter's lips let Finn know Turner had pulled the card he needed. Five years of playing poker together, and the man still could not hide his tell.

"Five seconds, Ward!"

Ward threw his cards down, rising from his chair. "All right, all right. I'm coming."

"Don't worry about your hand." Díaz grinned as she took his vacated seat. "I'll play for you."

"If you make me lose, I'm shaving *your* eyebrows."

Díaz snorted. "Come at me with a razor and see what happens."

Wouldn't happen. And not just because Díaz could kick any of their asses—the woman was crazy strong and sneaky— she always won whenever the crew sparred during morning workouts—but also because Ward was the worst poker player in the firehouse. Poor guy's tell could be seen from space.

"Raise or call?" Finn asked once Díaz glanced at Ward's abandoned hand.

"Raise."

She tossed a few chips in the middle pile. Turner eagerly upped the ante. Finn folded. Like that old song his dad used to sing, he knew when to hold 'em and when to fold 'em.

Bruiser sat up from her doggy bed in the corner of the station kitchen and started furiously barking. They didn't have an official firehouse dog, but since he'd adopted Bruiser, the little Yorkie mix had been the unofficial mascot. Everyone loved her, and with Finn living in a tiny studio apartment—

which sat unoccupied during his twenty-four-hour shifts—he brought her along to the firehouse.

"What is it, Bru, baby?"

The pup rushed over to him, sniffing his pocket. Leaning down, he stroked the little furball behind one floppy ear. As he reached in to pick her up, the tiny dog shoved her nose into his crotch.

"You ate the last sausage I had, you horker." His dog would eat until she couldn't move and then try to sneak one more treat. He had no idea where the little dog put it all. When she continued to sniff, he lifted her to his chest. "What is it, girl?"

The second he asked the question, his phone chimed with an incoming text. Bruiser whined, tiny legs whirling in the air, nose pointing down. This wasn't the first time his dog had known a call or text was coming. Weird. Maybe there was some high-pitched frequency that happened seconds before, which only dogs could hear.

Shifting Bruiser in his arms, he reached into his pocket and pulled out his phone, a smile curling his lips as he read the screen.

"Pru?" Turner asked.

He glanced up to his fellow firefighter. "How'd you know?"

The man shrugged. "You always get that sappy smile on your face whenever she calls or texts."

Finn scowled. "I do not have a sappy smile."

"You do, man," Ward called from his place at the sink.

Finn ignored his coworkers and focused on Pru's message.

P: *Are you free tonight to meet for dinner? We need to talk.*

Uh oh. The worst four words in the English language. Nothing good came after the phrase "we need to talk."

It was what you used when ending a relationship. But he and Pru weren't in a relationship. They were friends. You couldn't dump your best friend. Well, you could, but he didn't think Pru would ever "dump" him. They'd been through thick and thin together. Since the moment they'd met in middle school, they'd had each other's back.

He set Bruiser on his lap, and his thumbs flew across the screen, typing out a reply.

F: *Everything okay?*

He waited, holding his breath as the tiny dots finally turned into words.

P: *Yes. Everything is fine. I just have some important news to share with you.*

He breathed out a sigh of relief. He didn't know what he'd do if he ever lost Pru's friendship.

P: *So are you off tonight?*

He was. Normally he liked to stay at home the first night off-shift. Decompress. But Pru's text had his nerves on edge. He'd never be able to relax knowing she had something important to share with him.

F: *Yeah. In a few hours. I can meet you at City Tavern around six.*

P: *Sounds good. See you then.*

"Hey, Jamison. You okay?"

He glanced up to see Díaz staring at him, concern pinching her dark brows.

"Huh? Oh, yeah, I'm fine." If "fine" meant he was going to spend the next few hours worrying about whatever news

Pru had to tell him, then sure, he was fine.

Díaz did not seem convinced. "Everything okay with Pru?"

Ward walked back over to the table, drying his hands with a dishrag. "Man, I do not know how you stay just friends with that woman."

Tension had his back going stiff. "Pru's fine, and I stay *just* friends with her because she's awesome and I don't want to screw anything up."

Finn liked women. In fact, he loved them. But he didn't want anything serious. As a firefighter, he risked his life every day to save others. He loved his job, loved saving people, but he knew the dangers. In the course of his career, he'd lost a few good friends to the hazards of the job. That was a possibility he accepted. He'd accepted he might die in the service of others. He couldn't live with the chance of leaving a wife and kids to mourn him. He'd seen what that did to families, to futures.

Pru had always dreamed of white picket fences. A husband with a nine to five job, who coached Saturday little league. She and Finn were great friends, but they'd make a terrible couple.

"Hey," Ward finished drying his hands and tossed the dishrag into the station's laundry basket. "All I'm saying is Pru would make an excellent girlfriend, and I can't believe numbnuts over here doesn't see that."

He saw that. Hell, he knew how amazing Pru was. And he wasn't blind. She was beautiful—gorgeous, in fact. Her dark brown eyes always reminded him of rich, creamy chocolate. She was half a foot shorter than him, but it just made her easier to pick up and carry around, something she made him do whenever she got tired when they went hiking. Which was always. He'd never tell her, but it made him feel a bit like a superhero.

Her round face and slightly upturned nose gave her the appearance of one of those pixie things in that movie they'd seen as kids, the Spanish one where the monster had the creepy eyeballs in his hands. Finn had to sleep with the lights on for a week after watching it. And though she always complained about the static quality of her fine, chestnut brown hair, he thought it fit her perfectly, tightly pulled back and controlled in her trademark ponytail, but crazy and wild whenever she allowed herself to let it down.

Pru to a T.

"We're friends. End of story."

"As much as I hate agreeing with Ward on anything," Díaz said, ignoring the middle finger Ward sent her way, "I have to agree—even I think she's a catch."

"Ditto," Turner chimed in.

What the hell? Why were all his friends on his ass today?

"Aren't you married, Turner? To James?"

"Hey, just because I'm married doesn't mean I'm dead. Or stopped being attracted to other genders. Monogamy does not erase sexuality."

Finn shook his head. His coworkers were all crazy. He and Pru were friends. *Friends!* Men and women could be friends and nothing more, despite what every Hollywood rom com ever made said.

"Are we playing or what?" he asked.

His fellow firefighters shrugged, returning to the game. His eyes shifted to the clock as nerves cramped his stomach. Outside, he played it cool as Turner dealt a new hand, but inside, worry consumed his mind. This was going to be the longest end of shift ever.

• • •

Why was she so nervous?

Pru sat in a back booth at City Tavern, a bottle of locally made hard cider in front of her, its label shredded into a pile on the table. When she got anxious, she fidgeted, and her anxiety was so high right now even Mo's deep yoga breathing techniques couldn't help her.

She didn't understand. Why did it feel as if she was about to jump out of her skin? All she was doing was informing her bestie of her decision to use a sperm donor to get pregnant. It wasn't like she was asking for *his* sperm.

A flush heated her cheeks at the thought of Finn and sperm. Where had *that* come from? She didn't think of Finn and sex in the same sentence. Okay…maybe she'd had one or two inappropriate sex dreams over the years, but she'd also had a sex dream about Mr. Clean once, so her dreams clearly didn't mean anything.

It was just nervousness about discussing an important life decision with someone she held very dear manifesting in… strange ways. That's all. Finn was a guy, so of course her baby-obsessed brain would see his potential and subconsciously draw conclusions. Had to be it. No other reason.

"Hey, did you already order?"

She glanced up to see Finn smiling down at her. His sandy blond hair was slicked back, indicating he'd grabbed a shower before heading over. The dark gray T-shirt he wore clung to his muscles and showed off the colorful artwork covering his arms from his wrists to where the tattoos disappeared behind his sleeves. He'd once tried to convince her to get a tattoo, but she could barely handle the flu shot. No way could she sit still for hours while some sadist poked at her with a needle gun.

"Just a drink." She lifted her naked cider bottle.

Finn's dark blue gaze shifted to the pile of paper bits in front of her. His lips turned down, concern filling his face. As he took the seat across from her, he nodded to the pile.

"So, what's wrong? What did you want to talk to me

about?"

"Nothing is wrong. I just—"

"Hey, Finn." Laura stepped up to their table. "Need a drink?"

Finn smiled at the woman who'd become their regular server. Pru knew the younger woman was working on her pre-med degree at CU Denver. They always left her a generous tip to help her pay for school, and she always gave them top-notch service.

"Yeah, do you have any new IPAs?"

"We have a limited run of Naked Faust from 14er Brewing."

"Sounds good."

Laura left to get Finn's beer, and Pru chuckled softly.

"What?"

She lifted one shoulder. "You are such a hipster. You really need to branch away from IPAs at some point. There's a whole world of beer out there."

Her bestie lifted his hand to count on his fingers.

"First of all." His gaze fell to her cider. "Cider is the hipster drink for cretins who can't stomach a good hoppy drink. Second, I like supporting local brewers. And third, IPA is delicious."

Gross. She couldn't stomach the bitter drink. She preferred the crispness of a fruity cider. Not too sweet, zero hops, all delicious. It was a playful argument they'd been having for years now: beer versus cider. She supposed if all went well in a month or two, she'd be off alcohol for at least nine months.

Please, let everything go well.

Which brought her right back around to the reason she'd invited Finn out tonight. Operation: spill the baby news. Laura came back with Finn's beer and took their order of burgers and fries, and once she'd left, Pru knew it was now or never. Lifting her bottle to her lips, Pru took a deep, fortifying chug of cider.

"All right, now you're freaking me out." Finn's brow pinched. "What's wrong?"

"Nothing is wrong, I swear. But I do have big news."

The soft squeak of flesh gripping glass sounded in the air as Finn's knuckles turned white with the tense grip he had on his drink. A slight pinch of guilt turned her stomach. She hadn't meant to make him worry about her.

"Okay."

"You know how I've always wanted to be a mom?"

Finn nodded, lifting his beer to his lips. "Sure."

"I've decided to pick a sperm donor and be inseminated."

Beer spewed across the table, sprinkling her face with a fine mist of sour-smelling liquid as Finn snorted and choked on the sip he'd just taken. Pru jumped from her seat, rushing over to pound him on the back as he coughed and hacked the alcohol from his chest.

"Oh my God! Are you okay?"

"What *cough* did you *cough* say?"

She waited a moment, rubbing his back until the hacking and wheezing subsided then retaking her seat.

"I said I want to be a mother, and since all men suck—"

"Hey!"

"Present company excluded!" She gave him a sassy wink. "Most of the time."

He rolled his eyes but motioned for her to continue.

"Since it doesn't look like I'm going to find a life partner anytime soon, I've decided to become a mother on my own."

He sat there, a stunned expression filling his face, mouth slightly open in shock.

"I've already gotten approval from my doctor. I have enough in savings for multiple tries in case it doesn't work right away. Plus, I've talked with Lilly and Mo to ensure I can take time off after the baby is born. I've researched Head Start programs and applied for the waiting list on some very highly rated daycares. I'm prepared for anything—"

"Pru, Pru, Pru."

Finn leaned forward, grabbing her hands. She hadn't even realized she'd gripped her napkin and started nervously ripping the poor, flimsy paper into a pile of tiny flakes.

"I have no doubt you have researched, prepared for, and pro-and-con-listed every infinitesimal detail of solo parenting."

Most people might take his words as an insult, but Finn knew her, knew how important something like this was to her. She took it as the compliment he intended it to be.

"You are going to be a terrific mom."

Erratic nerves settled as warmth filled her. "Yeah?"

He smiled, the left side of his mouth lifting higher than the right. "The absolute best."

"Thanks, Finn." She let out a deep breath. "Wanna help me pick out a donor?"

• • •

Finn was going to need something a hell of a lot stronger than beer if he was going to help his best friend pick out a *sperm donor*. Now there was a situation he'd never in his life thought he'd have to deal with.

"You're only twenty-eight."

Pru stared at him as if *he* were the one who'd just spouted the most ridiculous thing ever.

"I'm aware of how old I am."

"I'm not saying you shouldn't go ahead with your plan, but aren't women having babies in their forties now? You could wait, see if you meet a nice guy."

Something strange and dark churned in his gut at the

thought of Pru meeting some guy and settling down to have a bunch of babies. She'd dated sporadically. He'd met some of the losers unworthy of his best friend. It wasn't that he begrudged her a nice guy. So why did the thought of another man in Pru's life always rub him the wrong way?

Her dark brown eyes turned sad. "Well, that's the thing. Remember when I thought Terrence and I were getting serious?"

Yeah, he remembered the prick who left because he got some fancy high-paying job out on the West Coast, breaking her heart. Good thing the asshole ran halfway across the country before Finn could break his nose in return.

"The douchebag? I remember."

Her lips curled up as she let out a small chuckle at his insult. "So, when I thought things were moving toward marriage and babies, I…I asked my doctor for a fertility test, and it turns out…"

She tugged on her ponytail, adjusting the already perfect hairstyle.

"I'm not going to bore you with all the medical jargon, but it appears I may not have as much time as the average woman. The longer I wait, the harder it will be, and since I haven't found any man who is up to my standards—"

"That's because your standards are impossible."

He loved Pru, but it was true. The woman held men to an almost unachievable ideal. Which was fine. In his opinion, no one was good enough for her, anyway. But damn, it really sucked that she had to move up her timeline. He knew how important having a family was to Pru and how much it crushed her when Terrence the Terrible left and destroyed the goal she'd been working toward. And now she had to move on to plan B all because of whatever biological issue stood in her way.

Good thing Pru always had a plan B…and C.

"Just because I won't sleep with anyone with boobs and a pulse doesn't mean I have impossible standards."

"Hey, I don't sleep with every woman I date." The rumors of his male prowess were highly exaggerated. "I'm just saying there are a lot of fish in the sea."

"Yeah, well, as I told Mo earlier, there's also a lot of garbage."

Fair point.

They were interrupted by Laura, who arrived at the table with two plates piled high with steaming hot french fries and burgers with all the fixings. Because he needed it for this conversation, Finn ordered another beer while Pru ordered another cider.

"So, tell me more about this process."

It might be weird, but he cared about her a lot. They weren't the kind of friends who said "I love you" to each other, but he did feel for her deeply the way one did for their best friend or a distant cousin you sometimes had wildly inappropriate dreams about.

This was a big deal. A huge, life-shifting decision, and he wanted her to feel comfortable sharing it with him. Even if it made him uncomfortable as hell. Talking babies and sperm donation with anyone was strange. Doing it with his best friend—his *female* best friend—well, that passed strange and flew straight into a bizarre world.

He sat there, eating his burger and fries, not tasting the food as his brain whirled and he listened to Pru talk about hormone levels, percentages and failure rates, ovulation tracking… Things he never in a million years thought he'd be discussing with her.

"You seem prepared." Overly so, but that was his Practical Pru. Never leaving anything to chance.

"Yup."

"And excited."

Pink lips curved upward, her entire being glowing. The weird tension he'd been holding in his muscles ever since she blurted out her news released at the sight of her delight.

This decision made her happy. That was all that mattered.

"I am." Lifting her cider, she took a drink, then frowned slightly as she placed the bottle back on the table. "Though, I will miss my cider. And sushi."

"And sex."

She snorted. "Can't miss what I'm not having. Besides, pregnant women can have sex. I'm pretty sure there's an entire section of the internet devoted to that particular fetish."

Talking babies was one thing, but he could not handle discussing porn with Pru.

"I think this news calls for a celebration." He bobbed his brow. "Shots?"

Pru arched one eyebrow. "We're not in college anymore, Finn. I don't want to be puking my guts out tomorrow."

"I won't let you puke." He caught Laura's eye from across the room and tilted his head, and the server gave him a nod and started heading their way. "But we need to celebrate your last hurrah before you saddle yourself with a kid for eighteen years."

"Hey!" She reached across the table to give him a very ineffectual punch to his shoulder. "Kids are not a saddle; they're a joy. Besides, I handle your childish ass all the time."

A chuckle escaped him. Man, he loved to rile her. "That you do. So, shots?"

Pru rolled her eyes, a smile tilting the corner of her mouth. "Okay, fine. One last celebration, but you're paying."

"Of course." He grinned as Laura arrived at their table. "Two chocolate cake shots."

"You got it." The server turned and headed toward the bar.

Pru raised a brow. "Chocolate cake shots?"

He shrugged. "Yeah. Celebration calls for cake."

She snorted. "Cake is made from flour, eggs, and sugar. We're going to be ingesting vodka, Frangelico, and lemon."

True, but it weirdly tasted just like chocolate cake, and wasn't that what really counted when celebrating?

"To Pru." Finn lifted his glass once Laura dropped them off. "Who is going to be the best mom ever!"

Her eyes misted over as she raised her own glass. "Thanks, Finn."

They clinked, biting into their sugared lemons before downing their drinks.

"Oh my." Pru gave a slight cough, wiping some sugar off her chin with the back of her hand. His gaze snagged on a few sparkling sugar crystals left on the corner of her mouth, and he had the strangest urge to lick them off.

What the hell?

All this *baby* and *sperm* talk was messing with his mind. Or maybe it was the shot. It had been a while since he'd indulged in anything more than a few beers.

"I haven't had one of those in a while. I forgot how yummy they are. And messy." Her eyes brightened. "Do we dare another?"

Loving the happy expression on his friend's face, he motioned to Laura for two more. "We dare."

Pru laughed. "Okay, I'm in. But I walked tonight, so if I get too sauced, can I crash at your place?"

His place was right across the street, and she'd bunked on his couch dozens of times when they'd both had a bit too much. Looked like tonight was going to be one of those nights. Knowing it might be the last "one of those nights," he tried not to let the small twinge of sadness interfere with the evening. Tonight was all about Pru, celebrating her news, supporting her decision.

"Of course, Pru. You know you're always welcome."

Laura dropped off their second shot, and Pru picked up her glass.

"Then here's to Finn, the best friend a girl could ask for."

He grabbed his own drink, clinking it with hers. "I am pretty awesome."

Dark brown eyes rolled upward, but her lips curved in a grin. "Whatever, egomaniac, just drink."

"To us." He raised his glass higher. "The most awesome best friends ever!"

"Damn right." She grinned, raising her glass to his. "To us!"

Chapter Four

One hour later, they stood outside the door to Finn's apartment, Pru clinging to Finn's back because the two-minute walk to his place had been too much for her. She blamed the three-inch wedges she was wearing. He'd blamed the third shot they'd taken.

Maybe he was right, but Finn had been the one to suggest shots in the first place, so he got to carry her tipsy butt back to his place. And if she took the opportunity to enjoy the warm, hard muscles of her bestie holding her up like her own personal superhero...well, she'd just blame that on the shots, too.

The sound of tiny nails and excited yips came through the closed door.

"Calm down, you crazy mutt." Finn released the grip he had on her legs and she slid to the ground as he reached into his pocket for his keys. "She must smell you, because she's never this anxious to see me."

Pru doubted it. She knew Bruiser loved Finn, but that didn't mean she wouldn't pounce on the opportunity to tease her friend.

"Naturally, because she knows I love her more."

Bright blue eyes narrowed. "Keep it up, Carlson, and I'll sneak into your apartment tonight and let Bruiser do her business in your shoes."

He would not. Mostly because Lilly would freak out if an animal of any kind stepped paw in their place. Their building was strictly pet free and there were hefty fines if anyone was caught hiding an animal.

She stuck her tongue out, pushing her way past him as he opened the door, only to be immediately assaulted by five pounds of fuzz trying furiously to jump into her arms.

"You want something to drink?" Finn closed the door behind her as Pru scooped Bruiser into her arms and headed for the couch. "I think I still have some of the pear cider you left from our last movie night."

"Just water is good." Her vision was fine, so she wasn't completely toasted, but her brain was kind of mushy. They'd downed three shots at the bar in addition to the cider she'd had with dinner. Not puke worthy for her by any means, but she was feeling a bit giggly, and that meant she was pleasantly tipsy and well on her way to drunk. More alcohol would be a bad idea.

He shuffled about in the tiny kitchen. Actually, "kitchen" was a generous term. More like a small fridge, sink, and stove shoved against one wall. Finn lived in a five-hundred-square-foot studio. His bed was on one side of the apartment, kitchenette on the other, and the only room, a small bathroom with sink, toilet and standing shower filled out the rest of the tiny apartment. He said since he was one person and he spent a third of his time at the station anyway, he didn't need a ton of room.

The lack of space became much clearer when more than one adult occupied the home, but since Bruiser couldn't come visit her per her building's rules, she didn't mind the cramped quarters to see the sweet pup. And Finn, of course. Plus, here they could watch all the trash reality TV they wanted. Lilly hated reality TV, so Pru rarely watched it at home.

"I think I have the latest *Single Woman Looking* on my queue if you wanna watch it?"

Speaking of trashy TV. "Load it up, Jamison."

Finn grabbed the remote, turning on the giant flat screen that took up a significant amount of wall space in his tiny home. He was such a guy. But she got to reap the benefits of his massive HDTV, so win, win.

"Who did she send home last week?"

Finn handed her a glass of water, taking a seat beside her on the small couch.

"Jayce. I think."

"Oh no! I loved Jayce. She should vote off Easton. That dude is an ass."

"Yeah, but he's good for ratings. I think the producers want to keep him on until the very end."

"Then how the hell is it her choice if the producers tell her who to pick to stay and go?"

He tilted his head her way, the corner of his mouth quirking up. "It's not real, Pru. Most of this shit is scripted or heavily edited. Everyone knows the relationships don't survive past the last cut."

She knew. It wasn't like she was some romantic hopeful like Mo or believed if two people matched perfectly on paper, they would last forever, like Lilly. She knew true love existed, but she was afraid it just didn't exist for her. Maybe that's why she liked these cheesy dating shows so much. She'd like to hold out some sliver of belief that some people could find lasting happiness with another person.

"Ah yes, I forgot for a moment I was watching with First Date Finn. Man who fears any commitment longer than the expiration date on his milk."

Since the couch was so small, their thighs were pressed together. Pru could feel, quite clearly, the tensing of Finn's muscles at her snipe. A small tendril of guilt wormed its way into her consciousness. They'd always teased each other, playfully of course, but that comment *had* been a little out of line. She knew the reason Finn never got serious with anyone had a lot to do with the dangers of his job.

"I'm sorry, Finn. That wasn't fair. Must be the booze talking."

His muscles relaxed a bit, the corner of his mouth lifting. "Oh, are we playing the blame it on the booze game now? Because if so, then can I say Easton is awesome and I'm glad he beat out Jayce?"

She gasped in mock horror. "You take that back."

He lifted his hands, chuckling. "Hey, it was the booze talking."

"You're gonna regret picking Team Easton."

Bruiser barked, a high-pitched yip, as Pru slid the dog off her lap and onto the floor before launching herself at Finn. She tackled him, slipping the ice she'd surreptitiously grabbed from her water glass down the back of his shirt. He shouted out a very creative four-letter word, jumping up and ripping his shirt off.

"Oh, you are going to pay for that, Prudence."

She laughed, reaching again for her water cup, but he was quicker. Finn dove, easily grabbing her and flipping her onto her back. Pressing her into the couch as he loomed above her, holding her hands high above her head.

"I think it's payback time." He reached for her glass of water.

"Finn, no! Don't you dare!" He raised the glass, condensation from the icy cold water running down in tiny rivulets on the outside. "Your couch! If you pour that water on me, it'll soak your couch."

One tattooed shoulder shrugged. "Couches dry."

She struggled as the laughter escaped her, but his hold was firm. "I'm serious. I don't want to get wet. I don't have anything to change into."

"We can always just hang out naked."

At his statement, her laughter died. All the playfulness was sucked out of the room as that one word hung in the air between them. A big damn elephant in a tiny room.

In that moment, she took stock of everything. Finn, shirtless, hovering above her with a firm yet gentle hold on her wrists, pressing her into the soft cushions of his couch. To a casual observer, this might look like lovers' foreplay. But they weren't lovers. They were friends.

She didn't want Finn.

So why was there heat pooling low in her belly?

Why did her breasts feel heavy and achy?

And why was there a trembling between her thighs?

Oh God. Did she want Finn? True, her best friend was attractive, but she'd never wanted to jump him. Not consciously anyway. So why now? Maybe it was the fertility drugs. Her doctor had mentioned they could affect her libido. Were the drugs making her see Finn in a new, sexually available light or was it the booze? There had to be some logical explanation for this sudden burning need, low in her gut, screaming for her to cross that forbidden line in their friendship.

"Shit, I'm sorry Pru." Finn shook his head, breaking the spell. "Forget I said that. Must be the booze talking."

He released her hands, lifting off her and heading toward the kitchen with her water, which he downed in one gulp.

"Bullshit."

It wasn't the alcohol. Yes, they were both a little drunk, but they weren't wasted or anything. The alcohol may have loosened his tongue, but it didn't plant the idea there in the first place.

"Look…" Finn tossed up his hands. "We're best friends and all, but I'm still a guy and you're beautiful, so yeah, I've thought about…you know, you and me naked a time or two, but I would never—"

"Wait, what?" Shock slammed into her, stealing her breath as his confession bounced around in her brain.

"Huh?"

She took a few steps forward. A few steps in Finn's place meant she was practically toe-to-toe with him now.

"You think I'm beautiful?"

His gaze rolled to the ceiling as if she'd asked the dumbest question in existence.

"You have mirrors, Pru."

Sure, but she'd never call herself beautiful. Cute, sure. In a girl-next-door kind of way. But she wasn't a sleek and sophisticated beauty like Lilly. Or a sensual bombshell like Mo. She was a solid seven. Eight if she got Lilly to do her makeup.

"I'm pretty, but I'm not—"

"You are more than pretty. You're a smoking hottie who would have all the guys on *Single Woman Looking* bending over backward just to get a special date night episode with."

Her heart pounded in her chest, palms going sweaty. Finn never said stuff like this to her. He never acted like he wanted anything more than what they had. And she'd never entertained the idea of her and Finn as anything other than friends. So why was her body suddenly throbbing with the need to know him in a way she'd never imagined? Why was there an ache between her thighs she knew only he could sate? Was it the booze? The pretty words?

Something else?

"I thought you said that show was fake."

"Ugh!" He scraped his hands over his face. "Can we

forget I ever said anything, please?"

No. No, they could not. Because now he wasn't the only one imagining the two of them doing the horizontal mambo. What did that mean?

"How long?"

"What?"

"How long have you thought I'm beautiful? How long have you imagined having…sex with me?"

"You've always been beautiful, Pru."

Oh. Well. That was just about the sweetest thing anyone had ever said to her.

Men had called her beautiful before, but none of them had ever known her the way Finn did. The compliment from him held such weight. He wasn't just calling her outer shell beautiful but all the stuff inside, too, because he knew the inside. Better than anyone.

When he called her beautiful, she felt it in her soul. A warmth that started in her chest and spread out through every inch of her body. Heating her blood. She *felt* beautiful, really, truly beautiful, in his eyes.

"And the sex?"

His hands reached up, locking behind his head. The movement made all the muscles in his chest flex. Her eyes flew to them. The ache between her legs intensified.

"This is the weirdest conversation ever," he said.

"How long, Finn?"

He blew out a breath, dropping his hands. "I don't know. There've been moments here and there for a while, I guess. Look, I'm not saying I want to switch from friends to dating or anything. I'm just admitting that yes, I have thought about having sex with you. Okay?"

A guilty expression crossed his face, but she didn't like it there. If she were truly honest with herself, with him, she'd had those thoughts, too. Ever since senior year when she noticed her bestie was kind of hot. Not that she ever did anything about it except for lock those weird feelings away in a box and shove it so deep down she'd never have to examine or reason them out.

Finn didn't want a family. He'd made his thoughts on the idea clear over the years. His job was too dangerous, and he couldn't put the worry of his possible death on a wife and kids. She understood that. Having lost her parents at such a young age, she commended her friend for his forethought. No child should have to lose a parent. It ripped a hole in you that could never be filled.

"I've thought about it, too." The words were out before she could realize she'd said them.

His head snapped up, eyes going wide. "You have?"

Now it was her turn to roll her eyes. "You're not exactly hideous. Some might even say you're hot."

The left corner of his lips lifted in a knowing grin. "Some?"

"Fine, me. I think you're hot. Happy now?"

He lifted one shoulder. "Kinda."

"So, I think you're hot and you think I'm beautiful and we've both had…curiosities about each other."

One pale brown eyebrow rose. "Curiosities?"

"What would you call it?"

"Sexual fantasies. Like a normal person."

Oh. Well then. Now she really wanted to ask him what *sexual fantasies* he'd had about her.

No. I want him to show me.

And why not? Maybe it was just the booze talking, but why couldn't they have one night of passion? They both knew this wouldn't go anywhere. They both had different life plans. So why not extend their celebration tonight from the drinking kind to the naked kind?

Do it! Have some wild monkey sex with the hot guy who

thinks you're beautiful!

The voice in her head sounded an awful lot like Mo, but she decided it made a solid point. They were attracted to each other, single, friends. She was sure that neither of them had any expectations of this turning into something more. It was just an itch they needed to scratch. A question that needed an answer. A desire that needed sating.

She took a step forward.

"Pru?"

She reached out, placing her hands on his chest. Holy cow, he was warm. So warm.

In all their years of friendship, she'd never touched his bare chest. Seen it, sure. They'd gone swimming together, worked out—when he dragged her ass to the gym, which was rare. But she'd never touched him like this before. With a clear intent that had nothing to do with playfulness or friendship.

Her fingers traced the Maltese cross tattoo over his chest. His heart beat a fast tempo against the pad of her finger as she followed the curved line of the fireman's hat in the middle, the straight lines of the axes behind, the bold typeface proclaiming *Fire Rescue* she knew he'd gotten one night with his crew to celebrate their solidarity to the job.

"Prudence," his voice growled, low and dark, full of heat, like nothing she'd ever heard before. "What are you doing?"

She had no clue, but damn if it didn't feel so very good.

• • •

His head was spinning, but he couldn't tell if it was from the booze or the touch of his best friend. She was killing him. Seriously, Finn was going to die of un-sated lust or a massive boner if Pru didn't stop her little sensual touchy-feely exploration right now. He was hanging on by a thin wire and she was playing with fire.

Silly Pru. That's my job.

Soft fingers traced the tattoo on his chest. How could a touch so light create such a maelstrom of sensation inside him? He and Pru touched all the time. Hugs, high fives: friend stuff. But this… She'd never touched his naked flesh before. At least not like this. Not with the hesitance of a new lover, the eagerness of unmasked desire. He knew why this affected him, because Pru was finally touching him the way he'd fantasized about. The way he'd never allowed himself to fully admit to wanting. Desperately.

Because they were friends, and friends didn't cross those lines.

Sure as hell looked like Pru wanted to cross some lines now.

"Pru, what are you—?" He sucked in a sharp breath as her delicate hand traveled downward, fingers trailing over his stomach and lower still until her hand rested on a very hard part of his anatomy.

"Oh my God," she gasped as she gently cupped him.

His body burned with need. Need for Pru. His hands flew out, automatically grabbing her hips and pulling her closer, trapping her small hand in-between their bodies. Her head tilted up, eyes closing in invitation. An invitation he would gladly accept.

Bending slightly, he captured her lips with his, a satisfied growl rising in his chest when her mouth opened on a gasp, allowing his tongue to plunge into the depths of her sweet, tempting mouth.

Her hand slipped from between them to wind around his neck. Perfect. Now he had better access to what he really wanted.

Moving his hands down to her ass, he grabbed two handfuls of glorious heaven and lifted. Pru, understanding his intent, eagerly complied by raising her legs and winding them around his waist as he stepped away from the counter. With their mouths still fused together, refusing to break for anything, even air—who needed air when he was kissing Pru?—he took the few steps to his bed and tumbled them down onto it. As they fell, Finn twisted, knowing the mattress was soft but not wanting anything to jar her. Not even a soft fall onto a cozy cushion.

Holy hell. He had no idea Pru could kiss like this. She was driving him mad. His body burned hotter than any fire he'd ever put out. Every nerve in him lit up with excitement and energy, as if he was a keg of gasoline and she was the damn match to spark him into an explosion.

Now he understood fire's scorching, hungry need to devour, because every bit of him screamed out its need to consume Pru.

Pru was amazing, she was unexpected, she was...*his best friend.*

The thought hit him like a bucket of water. Not cold water. Nothing could chill the raging inferno she'd ignited in him, but it did make him pause and pull back. What the hell was going on? Where was all this passion coming from? As he released her lips, she made an adorable little whimpering sound.

Much as he hated to kill the moment, he had to know. "Pru, what are we doing?"

She gazed down at him, dark brown eyes clear and filled with a burning need. A need for him. And hell, if that didn't make him feel ten feet tall.

She shook her head, gaze falling to his lips once more. "I have no idea."

"Well...as long as we're on the same page."

And with that, her lips crashed down on his once more. They stayed that way for minutes, or it could have been hours. Lips caressing, hands exploring. When she finally rose, sitting up on his lap, pressing down in just the right way to make his eyes cross, Finn knew they had to talk before things went any further.

What are you doing, dumbass?

He told his inner high school horndog to shut up. He was a grown ass man and he could control his impulses enough to make sure they were both aware of what they were doing before they crossed a line that might irrevocably impair their friendship.

"Pru, hold on." He grabbed her arms as she reached to take off her shirt.

She stopped, an impatient expression twisting her lips as she glanced up at him. "What?"

He tried to get the words past the giant lump of need in his throat. It was hard, but he managed. "How drunk are you?"

She paused a moment, considering his query before she shrugged. "Sober enough to know this is probably a dumb idea but drunk enough to want it anyway."

About the same as him, then. Still… "Are you sure you want to do this? Why now?"

Her head tilted, the way it did when she worked through a really big problem in her brain. He'd seen that look a lot during their honors algebra class. Pru was the only reason he'd passed. He also knew without Pru's instigation, he'd never be in the situation they were in now. Sure, he might have imagined it a time or twenty over the years, but he'd never have made a move. That always had to be her decision.

"I'm about to be celibate for eighteen years."

He laughed. "Single moms can have sex. They're called SMILFs."

She landed a light smack to his shoulder. "Don't be an ass."

At that, he squeezed his hands, which were currently on

her ass. "I'm just saying, you could get sex if you wanted to."

She shook her head. "It's not just about sex. It's about trust. I trust you, Finn."

His heart pounded so loud he was sure she could hear it.

"I know I seem like I have my entire life in control, planned out, and I do. I like it that way. When you have a plan, you can handle any obstacle thrown in your path—"

She was wrong. You couldn't plan for everything. Some obstacles could never be handled.

"—but before I tie myself down with late night feedings and sleep schedules, I want to know."

"Know what?" He held his breath.

"Know what it would be like. To lose myself, just for one night. To give myself over totally and completely to someone I trust. Someone I know will take care of me and give me everything I desire."

He would. Nothing on this earth would be more important to him than this. This task. This gift she was giving him.

But he didn't want her to wake up tomorrow and regret anything. It would kill him if, in a moment of weakened desire, they threw away years of friendship.

"I don't want this to ruin us." The fearful confession left his lips on a whisper.

She smiled, cupping his jaw with a gentle hand. "It won't."

"Are you sure?"

"Friends can have sex and still stay friends."

He scoffed. "I'm fairly certain there's about a dozen movies that prove that theory wrong."

"I didn't realize you were so well versed in Romcoms." She leaned down, brushing her lips across his in the barest of kisses. "We're solid, Finn. Nothing can break us. We're both consenting adults, and we know this isn't going any further than tonight."

"Things won't get weird?"

She shook her head. "No weirdness. I promise. Now, get those pants off, and let me see what the big fuss is all about."

"Oooh, I like it when you get all bossy on me."

She laughed as he rolled them over, rising from the bed and grasping the button of his jeans. He shucked his pants and boxers in one move, tossing the clothing across the room. He stood in front of Pru, aroused and at full attention.

"Hello, Finn's Fun Boy."

"Oh God, please don't call my dick that."

She giggled. "Well, can you blame me? Look at it!"

He'd rather look at her. Naked. She had far too many clothes on. He was starting to feel like this whole situation was a bit one-sided.

"So what nicknames do your good parts have?"

Her gaze drifted from his painfully hard erection to his face. "Good parts?"

He lifted one shoulder. "Let's start with the breasts."

"They don't have nicknames."

Bending down, he grasped the bottom of her shirt, tugging the soft material. "Good. Then I get to name them."

She lifted up, allowing him easier access to strip the shirt from her, leaving her in a simple beige cotton bra. She quickly rid herself of it in that magic way women had of removing undergarments before a man could blink.

"Well?" she asked, her hands twisting nervously in the bedding as she glanced at him, brown eyes filled with excitement.

"Magnificent." The word left him without a thought because that's exactly what she was.

He leaned down, capturing one stiff, peaked nipple between his lips. Pru cried out, grasping his head with her hands, pressing him closer, encouraging his movements. He spent long, delicious minutes worshipping the bounty that was her breasts before working his way down her stomach.

He paused at her hips, fingers quickly working the fastening of her jeans and pulling them down her legs.

"Shit," she muttered. "My underwear doesn't match."

Seriously? Did women think men cared about underwear fashion? He sure as hell didn't mind if she wore a beige bra with blue panties. As long as she gave him permission to take them off, she could wear polka dot boxers for all the shits he gave.

"You're beautiful, Pru."

She smiled at his compliment, lifting her hip in an invitation he would never refuse. His fingers tucked into the sides of her panties, drawing them down her legs and tossing them…somewhere. Who the hell cared?

The sharp yapping of a tiny pup permeated the thick fog of lust filling Finn's brain.

"Oh crap."

He turned to see Bruiser running in circles, a pair of blue panties covering her eyes.

"Oh no!" Pru covered her mouth, laughter escaping between her fingers as she stared at the poor, temporarily blind pup.

"Hold on one second." Finn stood, grabbing his wayward dog and lifting the clothing from her face. "Sorry, Bru Baby, but Daddy and Pru need some special adult time. How about I give you some treats and let you play in the bathroom for a bit?"

At the word "treats," Bruiser stopped barking, tongue hanging from her mouth in anticipation. Once he had his dog settled and happy behind closed doors, he returned to the bed.

"Now, where were we?"

"I believe you were right about here." She smiled, pushing his shoulders down.

He grinned, following her direction to the place he was

only too happy to go. He grasped her thighs, gently pulling them apart to settle himself in between, taking a moment to glance at the heaven that awaited him.

"Finn?" Pru's soft voice wavered hesitantly after a moment of his silent stare.

"I'm trying to think of a better word than magnificent, but I can't."

Her chuckles turned into a loud moan when his lips pressed to her center. Finn nearly lost his damn mind at the pure utopia that was Pru. He kissed, sucked, and explored every inch in front of him. He knew if he didn't get inside her within minutes, he was going to lose it. But not before she did. He wanted—no, *needed*—to make this good for her. Amazing. The best she'd ever had.

Her moans became louder. Breathing rapidly, he could feel how close she was. But not close enough. He slid a hand up her thigh, fingers joining in, delving inside as his tongue focused on the center of her need. In seconds she was crying out with release, nails digging into his shoulder. The sharp bite made him roar inside with pure male satisfaction.

"Holy shit, Finn!"

He chuckled, crawling up her body to relish in the view of the soft, warm flush on her skin.

"That was amazing," she said.

"It's not over yet."

His cock surged toward her, now resting precisely where it wanted to be. She arched against him, positioning her body so he slipped in, inch by inch. His damn head nearly blew off.

"Pru!"

Her hands slid down his back, grasping his ass and tugging, forcing him deeper inside. His mind blanked completely. Nothing in life had ever felt as amazing as being inside Pru. He shifted his hips, plunging in until he was fully seated. Something tickled in the back of his brain. Something important that he'd forgotten. But his mind was so consumed with Pru and the way she felt, the way she made him feel, that he quickly dismissed whatever tiny warning his lust-and-booze-filled brain was trying to communicate to him.

"Finn."

His name, a broken whisper on her lips. The sweetest sound he'd ever heard.

"More. Please."

Okay, second sweetest.

He moved, starting a slow tempo, but she arched her hips and pulled at him, demanding he go faster. Since he was hanging on by a thread as it was, he took his cue from her, increasing his pace, driving into her with a desperate need. One of her hands reached up, cupping his face. Her dark gaze stared into his, fire, need, passion, and trust all swirling in their depths. He'd never felt so turned on and humbled during sex.

"Pru." His voice came out as a growl. Her name. Nothing more.

He didn't have any thoughts in his head beyond her. She was everything at the moment. The beginning and the end.

She lifted her head, slipping her hand to his neck and tugging him down until their lips met. He knew he was close to losing it, so he slipped a hand under her hips, angling so every thrust hit her exactly where she needed.

In a matter of seconds, he felt her tighten around him, her lips wrenching from his as she screamed his name in delight. He continued driving into her, her cries forcing him over the edge as he gave one final thrust and joined her in the most astounding experience he'd ever had.

"You…" She panted, chest rising and falling with heaving breaths. "You totally lived up to the hype."

He laughed, kissing her softly. "Good to know. You, however, blew my fucking mind, Pru."

She grinned. "I am pretty awesome."

"That, you are." He rolled to his back, pulling her with him until she lay sprawled against his chest, tucked carefully into his side. "Stay?"

"I couldn't move if you gave me a million dollars." She opened her mouth in a jaw-cracking yawn. "My bones are jelly."

"Want me to carry you to the shower?"

She nuzzled against his shoulder. "As long as you hold me up in it, too. Between the booze and the orgasms, I think I've lost the ability to walk for the rest of the night."

He laughed softly. After rinsing them both in the shower, he carried a sleepy Pru back to his bed, tucking her into his side.

He kissed her brow softly. "Sleep, Precious."

"Night, Finn," she murmured, eyes already closed.

"Night, Pru."

He lay there for a while, listening to the sounds of her soft snoring, completely amazed by what had just happened and totally confused by the aching need in his chest to do it again.

Chapter Five

Pru roused into half consciousness as the warm weight beside her moved. She whimpered, annoyed that her pleasant cocoon of heat and peaceful sleep was being disturbed, plus that she had a mild headache. Stupid shots. Once she hit twenty-five, her tolerance for partying all night and popping out of bed the next morning had reduced drastically.

"Sorry, Precious. I have to take Bruiser out before her tiny bladder relieves itself over all my clean laundry."

Precious? Her brow furrowed at the new nickname. She didn't hate it, but it felt a little too…intimate.

More intimate than what you did last night? Her brain would have argued with her further, but then she felt Finn shift and leave the bed, tucking the covers—still warm from their night together—around her and slumber pulled at her satisfied body once more.

"I'll be back in a few."

Her mind drifted to sleep. Though she wasn't as muddled as Mo in the mornings, she didn't like rising before the sun, and since darkness still filled the small studio, she imagined the seven o'clock hour had yet to arrive. Pru slipped quickly back to dreamland where her mind played the most amazing dreams of her and Finn, naked. Only now she knew reality was so much better than anything her subconscious could conjure up.

She vaguely recalled Finn returning and slipping back into bed, tugging her into his warm embrace. Something small, but surprisingly weighty, covered her feet. Bruiser, she assumed. She burrowed into the cozy cuddles, her fuzzy, sleep-addled, slightly hung-over brain trying to tell her something important, but the slumber pulled and lulled her once more.

The next time she woke, the sun had risen, a bright ray spilling across her face from the window. Rather rude way to be woken up, but at least her headache was gone and she didn't have to wake alone. She was with Finn.

Oh my God. I slept with Finn!

All vestiges of sleep disappeared as the reality of what they'd done last night hit her like a proverbial ton of bricks. She'd had sex with her best friend last night.

She knew what his dick looked like.

She knew what it *felt* like.

What did this all mean? Her heart raced, panic gripping her. She didn't regret last night. Not one single second of it, but she had no idea what to do now.

She'd never had a one-night stand. Which was kind of what they'd agreed this was, right? Sating a curiosity. Scratching an itch. It wasn't like either of them planned to turn their friendship into a relationship. So where did that leave them this morning?

Did one-time sex only count at night or was it like a twenty-four-hour kind of deal? Did she stay and have breakfast? Run out claiming an important work meeting?

You can't say that, dummy; he knows you.

That was the problem. They knew each other so well. She usually knew what to do when she crashed over at Finn's place after a night of trivia or a movie marathon. They'd hit up Dozens for Novo coffee and a plate of Here's Your Aspen scrambled eggs, then walk down 16th Street Mall and people watch. But she'd always kept her clothes on those nights and slept on the couch, not in bed with him.

Could she sit across a busy breakfast diner chatting away with him now that she knew when he blew on his hot coffee, it was with the exact same gentle breath that rose goose bumps on her naked flesh just last night?

"Morning." His voice rumbled in her ear as he nudged the tip of his nose along her temple, leaving a soft kiss on her cheek. "Sleep okay?"

She turned to face him. Oh crap, it hadn't just been the booze. He was even sexier this morning than he'd been last night. Couldn't he have horrifying bed head or something? A small flaw for her to make fun of to get this strange panic out of her chest?

"Yup. You?"

The left side of his lips curled up in a grin. "Best sleep I've had in a long time."

Her too, oddly enough. She supposed good sex did that to a person. No. Not good sex—phenomenal sex.

"Sooooo, this is good. Fine. Totally cool," she said.

His smile faltered.

"I mean it's, you know, not weird."

"Okay."

She pushed her hair away from her face, fingers tugging on the strands. "'Cause we were wondering if it was going to be weird and, you know. It's not."

He raised one eyebrow. "Sure."

"Totally not weird." *Tug.*

The second eyebrow joined the first. "Right."

"Not weird at all." *Tug, tug, tug.*

He snorted. "Yeah, I'd be more convinced if you weren't commenting on how *not weird* it is. *That's* weird, Pru. And you're tugging on your hair."

Crap. The problem with sleeping with someone who knew you so well was you couldn't hide anything from them. Like an encroaching panic attack from the fact that *she slept with her best friend.*

"How's that freak-out going in there?" He reached out to poke at her forehead.

She swatted his finger away, scowling. "It's going just fine, thank you."

"Gonna run out on me or wanna grab breakfast?"

And there it was. He was offering her their agreement. One night of exploration and then everything back to normal. A wave of relief crashed over her.

They hadn't ruined anything. She didn't need to figure out what this meant or what she should do next. They were just Finn and Pru. Best buds, grabbing breakfast after a sleepover. Different from their usual sleepovers—naughtier, oh so naughtier. But he wasn't kicking her out or asking for more.

They were good.

They were them.

"If you think I'm running anywhere before I get some coffee and food in me, you're a bonehead."

"I've been called worse."

She laughed, starting to rise, but then the sheets slid against her skin, the sensual action reminding her of her lack of clothing. "Um, could you…?"

His eyes widened. "Seriously?"

"Yes, you perv! Close your eyes."

"Pru, I've seen it all. Seen it, touched it, tasted it—"

She smashed a hand over his mouth to stop the outrageous

words from escaping. Her cheeks burned, knowing everything he said was true, but unable to tamp down the embarrassment of it all in the light of day. Her best friend now had intimate knowledge of her. It was… Okay fine, it was freakin' weird.

His brow drew down, expression wary. Gently, he grasped her wrist and removed her hand from his lips. "You don't… regret anything, do you?"

"No!"

The denial came out a little too sharp and loud, but she'd hate it if Finn thought she regretted or resented him in any way. Quite the opposite. A tiny voice deep inside her was screaming for more. *More naked Finn time. Now!*

She shut that voice down. She had plans to attend to, and none of them involved adding benefits to the friendship with her bestie.

"Last night was…" She paused, trying to search for exactly how much it had meant to her without freaking them both out. "Perfect. I don't regret a single moment. Do you?"

He grinned. "Nope. Honestly, Pru. You kind of rocked my world. I knew all your exes were dumbasses, but I never fully grasped how much until last night."

Well, that was… She had no idea what that was, but it sure made her feel all warm and fuzzy inside. *Stupid insides, this is not the start of some fairy-tale romance. This was fantastic sex to tide me over for the next two decades.*

There. Inner nympho put in place.

"They were rather dumb, weren't they?"

"Any man who'd let you get away is a moron."

She sucked in a breath at his words. "You know this was a one-time thing, Finn."

His smile slipped, just the barest of a drop, but then his lips parted even wider, head shaking. "Um, yeah. We kind of went over that last night. I mean, I know we were a little bit toasted, but we talked about it. Or did Finn's Fun Stick cause you to have orgasmic amnesia?"

She shoved his shoulder. "Shut up—that's not a thing."

He laughed, rising from the bed, completely unashamed of his nudity, and headed toward the bathroom.

"Give me fifteen. I'm going to hit the three S's before we head out."

"Three S's?"

He glanced over his shoulder, grinning like a fool when he caught her staring at his ass.

What? She couldn't help it. Finn had a very fine ass.

"Shave, shower, and shit."

"Lovely."

Okay, now she knew they were back on solid friendship ground. You didn't talk about bathroom stuff with a lover. That was *annoying your friend* territory. Still, there had been that moment where she thought maybe he wanted more. Something in his eyes seemed almost sad when she reminded him of their deal.

No. That was crazy. Finn didn't want a relationship with her. He didn't want a relationship with anyone. He was First Date Finn. She was just out of sorts because of all that had happened.

The sound of a sharp bark caused her to glance down and see Bruiser at the foot of the bed, head tilted, tail wagging, tongue hanging out of the side of her furry little mouth.

"Hey, Bru. You want a treat?"

The tiny dog barked again, wagging her tail so enthusiastically that Pru was afraid it might just wag right off.

"Come on." She reached down, grabbing the sweet pup in her arms and tossing the covers off. "I bet I can get dressed and sneak you two treats before your daddy is done primping."

"I heard that!" a voice from the bathroom yelled.

"Finish your S's!" she yelled back.

True to their words, in fifteen minutes Finn was ready to go and Pru had dressed and fed Bruiser two treats. Since it was a nice, sunny day, Finn insisted they take his bike, even though the restaurant was less than a mile away. She agreed because she was starving and needed coffee...or maybe it was because holding Finn tight, feeling the vibrations of the rumbling motorcycle, conjured up memories of last night.

No. It was the coffee thing.

Yup. That was her story and she was sticking to it.

Breakfast went off like usual, with a few awkward moments here and there. Honestly, she'd be more worried if there *weren't* a few strange bits. It wasn't like she wanted Finn to fall madly in love with her or anything, but she did want last night to mean something to him.

It meant something to her.

After breakfast, he dropped her off at her apartment building. She slid off his bike, handing him the spare helmet, which he stashed back in the side bag.

"I'm on shift starting the day after tomorrow, but shoot me a text whenever."

"Will do."

There was a moment. A pause in their goodbye that normally didn't happen. Under ordinary circumstances she would wave, turn, and head inside. But last night had been anything but ordinary. It seemed they were still trying to find their new footing, even though they'd agreed not to let what happened change their friendship.

You dummy! her brain screamed. *Sex always changes everything.*

It didn't have to. They could be two mature adults about this. So why wasn't she leaving? Why wasn't she waving? Why the hell was she moving closer to Finn and why was he grasping the back of her neck and pulling her to him?

He tugged her closer, and she came to him, like a moth

drawn to an irresistible, dangerous flame.

His head tilted, lips pressing against her own. She opened for him instinctively, allowing his tongue to slip inside. She moaned, deepening the kiss at that first electric spark of his tongue caressing hers. Then, all too quickly, it was over, and he was pulling away.

"See ya, Pru."

"See ya, Finn."

Then he was gone. Pulling away on that ridiculous excuse for a vehicle. Leaving her wondering what that was. They'd said sex wouldn't change anything, so why did he kiss her goodbye? Friends didn't say goodbye with their lips. Okay, so they did, but not in a tongues-down-each-other's-throat kind of way.

She headed into her complex, pondering what had just happened and what she should do about it as she made her way to her apartment.

Nothing. She should do nothing because they agreed on as much.

That was just a goodbye kiss. A 'thanks for the great night' kind of thing. Right? She didn't need to think about it or talk about it with anyone. She could just put it in her nice memory box in her brain and move on.

Mind made up, she opened the door to her apartment to be greeted by the sight of Mo and Lilly at the kitchen table going over seating charts.

"I slept with Finn!"

Stupid self! We weren't supposed to tell anyone.

Oh God, she couldn't keep it in. She needed to tell someone, talk about it, analyze what the hell just happened. Who better to do that with than her two closest friends? Well, her two closest friends who she hadn't just slept with, that is.

"What?" Lilly pushed her glasses up her nose, shock dropping her jaw wide.

"Hell yes! I knew it!" Mo pumped her fist in the air, jumping up and doing a little booty shake dance around the table. "Come here, sit. Tell us everything."

She allowed her roommates to ply her with coffee and cookies as she poured out the entire tale. Minus some of the more private details.

"I knew it," Mo crowed again, a smug grin on her face. "I knew you two would hook up eventually."

"So, what now?" Lilly asked, concern marring her brow.

"Nothing now." At her friends' confused stares, she continued. "It was a one-time thing. We both agreed. I have plans, baby plans, and Finn doesn't want anything like that. His job is too dangerous. Too much risk of putting any potential wife and kids through trauma if he were to…" She swallowed past the lump in her throat. She knew Finn's logic was sound because if he ever died in the line of duty, it would gut her.

And she was just his best friend. She couldn't imagine what it would do to any wife or children he had.

"We just had to see, I guess. What it would be like. Now it's out of our systems and we go back to just being friends."

Mo and Lilly shared a skeptical glance.

"Seriously, you guys. It's fine."

Mo crossed her arms over her chest. "Then why did you tell us?"

Because she didn't like keeping things from her friends. "I don't know…bragging rights?"

Lilly shook her head. "One night with Finn and you turn into a frat boy."

"Finn was never in a frat."

"Yeah, but he was in *you*. Last night. Heigh-oh!"

No one high-fived Mo, so she raised her other hand and slapped fives herself.

"My humor is so underappreciated around you two."

"Can we just move on from this, please? I don't even know why I brought it up. Let's just get to work."

Lilly glanced over at her and tilted her head. "Why don't you go grab a quick shower and change of clothes? When you're done, you can meet us downstairs and we'll go over the Marlowe-Hillard wedding. They finally decided on a venue, so they'll be sending us a deposit check soon."

Pru breathed a sigh of relief. Thank goodness for Lilly who was always ready to put off emotional stuff and dive into work. Work would distract her from whatever weirdness was going on between her and Finn right now.

After the venue was set, things tended to take off pretty quickly from there. The Marlowe-Hillard wedding wasn't for another eight months, but things in Denver tended to book up fast. The couple was smart to lock down their location now.

It was time to work. She couldn't ruminate on last night's drunken escapades, no matter how good they'd been. Her mind drifted to last night. And the way Finn had seemed to know what she wanted, what she needed, even before she had.

How?

Had their years of friendship formed a connection that spanned into the bedroom or was he just that good?

Ugh. She had to stop thinking about it. It was over. Done. A nice memory to bring out on a cold, lonely night, but not one to analyze to death.

It happened and it was over. Their friendship remained. Last night would soon be nothing but a pleasant memory for them both. It had no lasting effects.

None at all.

Chapter Six

"Prudence C.?"

Pru looked up from the puzzle blaster game she'd been playing on her phone to the nurse calling her name. This was it. Today was the day. Well, not *the* day, but the important first step day. Over the past week, she'd been working with her roommates on their upcoming winter weddings, and at night she'd narrowed down her pro and con list to one winning donor.

I'm the one who's really winning.

Because she was on track to get her baby. Hopefully. If everything worked out. Today she was here to have some blood work done and get her hormone levels checked.

"Come on back."

The nurse smiled as Pru rose from her seat and moved through the waiting room door into the back where the exam rooms were located.

"Okay, Prudence, I'm just going to need weight and a urine sample, then we can head into the room."

After stepping on the scale and taking a moment in the

small bathroom to pee in a cup, Pru followed the nurse into an exam room where she had her temperature and blood pressure taken. Next, she was sent to the phlebotomist to have her blood drawn and finally, back into the exam room to wait for her doctor. All the while, her heart raced. It was happening—she was on her way to becoming a mommy. She knew there might be hurdles and failures ahead, but right now the excitement outweighed any impending disappointment.

She sat on the high exam table, the crinkle of the sterile paper filling the quiet room with each tiny movement she made. Plans and dreams came to life in her head as she stared at the various posters displaying the female reproductive system, with the sharp sting of antiseptic and cleaner assailing her nostrils with each anticipatory breath.

A light tap sounded on the door.

This was it! Her journey was about to begin.

"Come in."

The door opened and Dr. Richardson stepped through. The middle-aged woman smiled.

"How are you today, Prudence?"

She smiled back at the doctor helping her achieve her dreams. "I'm fine, thank you."

"Great. I understand you've chosen a donor."

"Yes, it was a tough decision, but I think I picked the perfect candidate." She hoped. The probability of her screwing up as a parent at some point in her child's life was a guarantee, but she hoped she would at least start out on the right foot with a perfect donor selection.

"Wonderful." Dr. Richardson smiled. "Let me just have a look at your chart and we can see how everything…"

The doctor's words fell away, her dark brow furrowing as she glanced at Pru's chart.

"Huh, there appears to be a slight issue."

Her heart jumped into her throat, clogging the airway,

making it impossible to breathe. Dreams started to crash around her, shattering before they'd even had a chance to actualize.

Calm down, she simply said issue *not* impossibility. *You don't know what's going on. Chill out and ask.*

Sucking in a deep breath, she listened to her inner self and pushed down her fear. Clearing her throat, she tried her best to sound cool and collected as she asked, "Was there a problem with one of my tests?"

Please say no, please say no, please say no.

"No."

Oh, thank goodness.

"No problem, but it appears from your urine sample and blood work that you don't need a donor after all."

What? Of course she needed a donor. How could she not need a—

"You're pregnant."

"I'm...what now?"

"Pregnant. Just a few weeks along. When was the start of your last cycle?"

She struggled to think of anything at the moment, let alone the first day of her last period. She was pregnant? Somehow, she had the cognitive ability to open up the cycle app on her phone and relay the important information.

"Okay." The doctor wrote something down on the chart. "So, conception likely would have happened two weeks ago. Have you had any new sexual partners?"

Two weeks ago? Then that meant...

Oh no.

No, no, no, no, no.

She didn't know why she was bothering to do the math or was surprised by the realization. There was only one person she'd had sex with in the last *year*. One person she'd celebrated with, gotten drunk with, thrown caution to the wind with.

And, now she realized, in her inebriated state that night, had forgotten to secure some form of birth control with.

There was only one option. Only one answer.

She was sitting in a fertility clinic, pregnant with her best friend's baby.

Pru sat in her car in the parking lot of her apartment building. She didn't remember driving here. She didn't remember leaving the doctor's office. After Dr. Richardson came in and dropped the baby news on her, she'd gone blank. Going through the motions, listening to explanations and instructions, then somehow, she'd arrived here. At home.

Pregnant, but not in the way she expected. Not in the way she'd planned.

It happened. It's done. Plans change.

This was a pretty damn big change.

Nothing to do now but move forward. Put one foot in front of the other and make a new plan. First step of the new plan was getting out of the car.

She opened the door, sliding out and shutting it behind her. *Step one accomplished.* Now onto step two: entering her home and telling her friends.

"Come on, feet." She glared down at her motionless appendages covered in a pair of comfortable black pumps. "Move. You know how it works. First right then left. Or left then right. I don't care how you do it, girls, just get a move on."

And now she was talking to her feet like a weirdo. Could she claim pregnancy brain this early on?

After a moment of silent pep talks, she finally mustered up the courage to make the twenty-foot walk to her complex door. Forgoing the elevator—because she already felt suffocated enough as it was, no need to add a tiny moving death box to the situation—she hoofed it up the two flights of stairs. The brisk incline made her already racing heart pound louder, the sound filling her ears until all she heard was the relentless beating of her consciousness screaming:

I'm pregnant! I'm pregnant! I'm pregnant!

Reaching her apartment door, she flung it open. The words blocked out every other ambient noise.

"I'm pregnant!"

Wait, had she screamed that out loud? A quick glance to the shocked expressions on Mo's and Lilly's faces confirmed, yes. Yes, she sure had.

"Well." Mo tilted her head, blond hair dyed with green and pink streaks this week, spilling over her shoulder. "That was fast. I thought you had to do some tests and stuff. Can they tell right after turkey basting you?"

A groan escaped her lips. She shut the door—slammed might be the more accurate term—and flung herself into one of the kitchen chairs.

"How many times do I have to tell you? There's no turkey baster involved. It's a medical procedure performed in a sterile environment with hospital-grade equipment. Not kitchen utensils."

Flopping her purse down on the table, she pulled out the folder on pregnancy the doctor had given her. What medications were safe to use, what to look out for, general nutrition information, a whole host of things she already knew because she'd done her homework. But apparently, they gave the same packet to all expecting parents.

Expecting parent.

She was going to be a mommy! She might be in a tailspin right now over the exact way it had happened, but the shining light in all of this was that she got her wish, her dream. She had her baby. Or would have, in nine months, technically.

"And besides, I didn't have the procedure," she continued. "Because yes, I did have some tests to run, and those tests revealed I'm already pregnant."

"Wahoo!" Mo pumped her fist into the air with a smile. A smile that faded after a moment. "You don't look happy. Why don't you look happy? I thought this was what you wanted?"

"It is, but…"

"But it didn't happen the way you planned," Lilly confirmed.

"Plans are overrated." Mo shrugged. "I say, go with the flow."

"And that's why you don't handle the business finances or schedules." Lilly gave Mo some serious side eye. "I assume she's upset because of who the father is."

"What? Why would she be upset the dad is…" Mo's jaw dropped. "Oh my God, it's Finn! It has to be!"

Pru didn't know if she was insulted by her friend's gleeful smile at discovering the truth or relieved that she didn't have to reveal it herself.

"Of course it's Finn. Who the hell else would it be?" It wasn't like she had a long list of lovers. Or any other than him recently. "And I'm not upset." She glared at Mo. "I'm just… This…this wasn't the way it was supposed to go."

Mo shrugged. "Plans change."

She knew. She'd said the same damn thing to herself ten minutes ago.

"What am I going to do?" She slumped, head falling to the hard oak table. *Ouch!*

"Have you told him?" Lilly asked gently.

She tilted her head to the side, tugging on her hair as she avoided eye contact with Lilly. "No. I came straight home after finding out. What was I supposed to do, text the guy who never wants kids with 'Hey Finn remember that one night we got kinda drunk and crossed a line in our friendship? Well, guess who's going to be a daddy!' Oh, this can't be happening."

Curly, multicolored hair filled her vision as Mo crouched beside her.

"But it is happening, isn't it, little zygote? Who's got a funny conception story? You do, you adorable little one. Who was the strongest swimmer? You were, yes, you were."

"Mo, stop talking to my stomach like it's Bruiser or I will put black dye in your shampoo."

"You. Wouldn't. Dare." Her roommate snapped upright, gathering her cherished locks in her hands. "And anyway, I was just trying to lighten the mood. This is a good thing, Pru."

"How?" She sat up, staring at her friend. "How is this a good thing? Finn doesn't want kids. He's never wanted kids. He's always said so. How is he going to be happy about this?"

"Because you're happy." A smile warmed Mo's face as she reached out to grasp Pru's hand. "You two are friends, and friends are always happy if one of them gets their heart's desire. Think of how happy it will make Finn to know he gave you what you wanted most."

She really wished she could look on the bright side of this like Mo, but the woman was an eternal optimist. She never saw the downside to anything.

"While he might not be as delighted as Mo might assume," Lilly said, gripping Pru's other hand, "I do agree that Finn will be happy for you. I know we are."

A sheen of moisture blurred her vision. Hormones already? No. Just amazing friends. She blinked back tears, so ridiculously grateful she had these two in her life.

"But he never wanted to be a father."

"And he won't be." Lilly nodded. "You wanted to be a mom and you're willing to do it alone. Why should that change?"

Why indeed? There was nothing saying she and Finn had

to get married or anything. It wasn't medieval times.

"But what if he thinks I tricked him? I mean, to get pregnant."

Both women laughed. She didn't find it funny. It was a legitimate concern.

"Pru, honey." Mo patted her hand. "You are a terrible liar. You couldn't trick a cat into a paper bag."

Hey! She could, too. Probably. Maybe. If there was catnip in there, she was sure the furry beast would go in.

"Did you tell him you were on the pill?"

She shook her head at Lilly's question. "No."

"Did he mention anything about condoms or protection of any sort?"

Another shake. "We, um, had a few shots at the bar and kind of got so wrapped up in…things, I guess it just slipped both of our minds. To be honest, I didn't even realize we forgot the condom until today. When I found out. I guess drinking like we were twenty-one-year-olds on spring break wasn't the best decision."

Mo whistled. "Bad decisions make great stories."

Fantastic, she could tell her future child they were a drunken mistake. That wasn't how she planned this to go. The idea had been to sit them down one day and explain how she wanted them so much she carefully selected their donor, not got drunk and jumped her best friend.

"You were both drunk, you both forgot protection." Lilly squeezed her hand. "So, no one trapped anybody. And Finn wouldn't think that anyway, sweetie. You know he wouldn't."

True. The errant thought must have come from her panic or shock. Finn knew her better than anyone. He'd know this was as much of a shock to her as it would be to him. Once she finally told him.

Oh crap, how the hell was she going to tell Finn?

"I have to tell him."

"Duh."

She glared at Mo, who held up a hand in surrender. "Sorry, just pointing out that this would be too big a secret to keep. Secrets are like cancer—they spread, infecting every ounce of goodness and light in a person. They're evil."

It wasn't like she could keep a secret from Finn anyway. She never could. And certainly not one this big.

"I should text him, find out when he's off shift."

Because there was no way in hell she would drop this bomb on him at work. She wasn't a monster. They needed to talk about this. Really talk, without his fellow firefighters present or the risk of him getting a call and running off to an emergency.

She had no idea what they were going to do. She wanted to be a mom and Finn had never shown any burning desire to be a dad, so maybe this would work. She could carry on her plan of single motherhood like always, just with a donor she was familiar with.

Much more familiar with.

"Do you want to plan out what you're going to say?"

From anyone else, that might sound sarcastic, but she knew Mo was serious. Her friend knew her, knew Pru would want to go in with a plan, like she did with all things in life.

Barring one particular night about two weeks ago.

"I think it might be wise to jot a few things down."

Lilly patted her hand, rising from the table. "I'll go make you a cup of peppermint tea."

She really had the best friends/roommates/business partners in the world. And she was incredibly grateful all this happened during their slowdown season. Then again, she might not have lost her head over Finn during springtime. They would have been so slammed with weddings, she wouldn't have had the time to go over to his place and lose her self-control. And her panties.

"Here's a pen and notepad."

She glanced up at Mo and Lilly. Her sisters at heart. Tears welled again, but this time she did nothing to stop them.

"Thank you both, for...everything. For supporting my original plan, for being excited about this twist, for having my back no matter what."

"Of course, sweetie. We always have your back. We love you," Lilly said.

"Yeah, we're the three musketeers," Mo added.

She laughed through her tears. "Pretty sure those were dudes, Mo."

"Fine, then we're the Sanderson sisters. Y'know, minus the evil witch part, but totally with the diva Bette Midler part."

She stood and opened her arms.

"Oh yay! Hug time."

Mo gleefully threw her arms around Pru, carefully squeezing her. Lilly set down the tea box, dutifully coming over to join the display of affection she rarely took part in. For Pru, because she loved her, and so did Mo, and Pru loved them back with all her heart.

"Pru?"

"Yeah, Mo?"

"Can I rub your tummy?"

"Only if you promise not to talk to it like my baby is a dog."

"I don't think the baby has ears yet," Lilly said, pulling away from the hug after her allotted five seconds of affection.

"Then I won't talk. I'll just send it all my love and positive energy to grow into a big, strong, healthy baby who will be spoiled by its auntie Mo when it's born. Yes you will be, honey."

Mo placed her hands on Pru's stomach even though there was no bump there yet. And still, a warm rush of happiness settled over her at her friend's touch. She knew a lot of pregnant women didn't like people touching their bellies, but to Pru it reinforced the culmination of a dream.

Her baby.

Plans had changed, but Pru was lucky. She had the two best friends in the world standing by her side. And, hopefully, another one who—after he got over his initial shock—would be just as happy and supportive of her.

One thing she knew for sure—this was definitely changing everything.

Chapter Seven

Finn shoved the last of the half-eaten pizza in the trash. He was pretty sure it had been pizza at one point. Hard to tell what was really under all that fuzzy green stuff growing on top of the weeks-old meal he'd forgotten about. That's what happened when you spent days away from home. He'd just finished his twenty-four-hour rotation and now had two days at home to relax and unwind.

He needed it too.

They'd been called to the scene of a nasty car wreck. Worst he'd seen in a long time. Night before last, they'd gotten a typical early Colorado snowstorm. Nothing big, just a few flurries and a severe drop in temperature. Happened every November. But the sudden chill and the wet snow had created a black ice situation on the roads. People tended to forget how to drive safely for icy roads over the summer.

Late in the night they'd gotten a call for a five-car pile-up near the Cherry Creek Mall. Three cars completely totaled, six people sent to the hospital with broken bones, concussions, lacerations, and one poor soul headed to the morgue. Sadly, there hadn't even been a chance to save the woman. She'd died on impact.

Damn. Sometimes he hated his job. When he couldn't help.

A sharp bark caused him to glance down and see Bruiser sitting at his feet, head tilted in that way she looked at him when she sensed his unease. Her tiny paw scraping his foot like a little doggo pat.

"Hey, Bru Baby." Bending down, he scooped her up into his arms, allowing her to attack his face with sweet puppy kisses. "How do you always know when I need love? Such a smart girl."

He'd never understand people who didn't like dogs. His fur baby was the best. On days like today, when he just felt so helpless and raw, her unconditional love and instinctive understanding made the pain a little easier to process.

His cell pinged with an incoming text message.

P: *You off today?*

The darkness faded even more as he read the question from Pru.

F: *Yup. Just got off a few hours ago. Wanna hang?*

Over the past few weeks things between him and Pru had been...off. They'd been texting, hung out a few times. But there had been no discussion of their night together. They both avoided bringing up the topic, and at times he felt like he was walking on eggshells around Pru. He didn't like it. One of the things he cherished most about their relationship was their ability to talk openly and honestly about anything. But their drunken one-night stand was apparently something they were brushing under the rug to pretend as if it never happened.

He refused to examine why that thought caused a little ping of sadness to hit him square in the gut.

His eyes focused on the three little dots, indicating she was typing, for what seemed like forever.

"Gee, Pru, composing an essay?"

Bruiser barked in his arms at the mention of her other favorite human. He waited, wondering what long and complex message his friend could be sending his way. Then the text finally came through.

P: *Yeah.*

Huh. Maybe there'd been a connection error or something.

His thumb flew over the screen as Bruiser settled into the crook of his left arm.

F: *Grab dinner at Benny's?*

Her response came much faster this time.

P: *How about I grab takeout and bring it over after I finish up some work stuff? Around six?*

Worked for him. Though he was feeling better, he still wasn't in the emotional state to be around a huge, noisy crowd of people. It always took him a little bit to recover from a fatality scene.

F: *Sounds good. See u then.*

P: *Later.*

Finn spent the next few hours making sure the place was picked up—which took all of thirty minutes in the tiny space—taking Bruiser out to the dog run down the street for some playtime and then hitting the shower. He'd just finished getting dressed when a soft knock sounded on his front door.

Bruiser went crazy, barking like a dog possessed.

"Calm down, Bru."

The pup didn't listen, instead increasing her yips as he opened the door to reveal Pru holding a sack from which mouthwatering smells of cheese and spices emanated.

"Did you get me enchiladas?"

"Yup. And the steak fajitas."

His stomach growled in anticipation of the best Mexican food Denver had to offer.

"You are a goddess. I am not worthy of your friendship."

"True." She laughed, handing over the bag and stepping inside. "But you got it anyway."

Lucky him.

"Hey, Bruiser," Pru cooed to his small dog, who was currently attacking her leg with puppy kisses. "How you doing, girl?"

Pru bent down as he closed the door behind her. Bruiser hopped into her arms, the dog's tiny wet nose sniffing like crazy. Probably smelled the food on Pru's coat. He had no idea where his small pup put the endless stream of food she consumed.

"Want to watch something while we eat?"

"Um, actually, can we talk first?"

He nearly dropped the food but managed to keep hold of the bag and deposit it on the coffee table. *Can we talk* was never followed by anything good. From anyone. He turned to see Pru standing just inside his apartment, a slight frown marring her face.

"Is something wrong?"

She hugged his dog tight to her. Bruiser had nudged her face into Pru's midsection, sniffing around like the woman had bacon in her pockets or something. Crazy dog, didn't she know he had all the food?

"No, I mean, yes. I mean…maybe?"

How could something be maybe wrong?

"Come here." He held out his hand, and she came willingly into his embrace. Bruiser yipped when he accidently squeezed too tight, squishing the tiny dog between them. "Sorry, Bru baby."

He pulled back to stare down at Pru's worried face. For one moment, her familiar features morphed into the face of the poor woman who'd died in the crash. He shook his head, banishing the image. It happened sometimes. When he experienced a traumatic scene, the images popped up at unexpected times. He was still decompressing. Death, even the death of a stranger, left an impact.

As hard as it was for him, he knew it was a million times worse for the poor woman's family. The exact reason he didn't want a family of his own. He'd seen the devastation losing a loved one caused first hand. But Pru wasn't dead on the pavement somewhere. She was fine. Here, in his apartment. Worried about something, but not dead.

"No matter what it is, everything will be okay."

"I know." She took a deep breath, stepping back. "Have some food first. Then we'll talk."

Right, like he'd be able to eat one bite now knowing something was bothering her. But bodily functions sometimes trumped nerves, and somehow Finn found himself devouring the delicious meal in less than ten minutes. Pru had her usual beef and bean burrito, which she ate while sneakily feeding bits of meat to Bruiser, who had yet to leave the woman's lap.

"You want a drink?"

She held up her bag, pulling her water bottle out from the side pouch. "I'm good."

"Okay, so what did you want to talk about?"

"Right, um, hold on."

She dug through her purse, rifling about in the cavernous

depths. He wondered what she could be searching for. For all he knew, she had a full cheesecake in there. He'd dug through that thing before in search of gum. He never found the gum, though he had found bandages, pens, a notepad with various numbers and calculations on it, a half-eaten granola bar, hand sanitizer, one of Bruiser's chew toys, and a couple of tampons, which he first mistook for candy.

She laughed for a solid ten minutes when he asked if he could have one. He didn't think he'd ever live down that embarrassment. But in his defense, he grew up with four brothers. How was he supposed to know what a tiny, packaged to-go feminine product looked like?

"Crap!" she exclaimed, but the curse was muffled by the bag. "Where is it? I had it all written down."

She'd written down what she wanted to say to him? It must be important.

"I can't be losing my mind already—it's only been a few days."

"Pru." He placed a hand on her shoulder, pausing her frantic searching. "Just tell me what's up."

Abandoning her bag of mysteries, she glanced up, determination replacing the panic. There was his Pru.

Nothing could faze her for long. Not even losing whatever well-planned speech she'd prepared for him. Though why she thought she needed to plan out what she wanted to say was beyond him. They were best friends. She could say whatever she wanted. No planning required.

Could be about that night.

He swallowed the panic rising in his chest. Did she regret it? Want a repeat? Want to wipe it from his memory and pretend like it never happened? Honestly, he wasn't sure which option freaked him out more.

"Okay, here goes." She closed her eyes, taking a deep breath before opening them again and staring straight at him.

"I'm pregnant."

"Oh." A myriad of emotions flew across his synapses in a matter of seconds: shock, happiness, worry, sadness. He wasn't sure why that last one was in there, but he ignored it and focused on the most important one. "Congratulations! I didn't even know you'd picked a donor yet."

"I didn't." She shook her head. "I mean, I did, but I didn't get to use his…um…donation."

"Huh?"

Now he was confused. He knew she was planning to get inseminated—still a weird thing to know about his best friend—but how could she be pregnant if she hadn't picked a…

Oh shit.

The reality of the situation sunk in.

Pru's nervousness, her need to talk, the planned-out speech… She wasn't just pregnant, she was pregnant with—

"You mean, I'm the… You and me… We…" Apparently the only thing it took to turn him into a blubbering moron was knocking up his best friend.

Knocking up.

His best friend.

She nodded, smoothing down her ponytail the way she always did when she was nervous. "Yeah. I guess in the, um, excitement of everything, and with the alcohol, we kind of forgot about protection."

Damn. He'd never forgotten the rubber before, but now that he thought about it, he couldn't remember using one or asking about birth control. He'd just been so lost in what had been happening, it completely slipped his mind. And, yeah, he might have had one shot too many. The logistics of how they'd gone from watching TV to naked in his bed that night were a little hazy.

"Shit, Pru. I am so sorry. I never forget. I swear. And I'm

clean. I just had my physical a few months ago, and I haven't been with anyone except you since, and—"

"Finn, stop." She held up a hand. "I know. I don't blame you. Honestly, for a second after I found out, I was worried you might, um, blame me. Think I was using you to get a baby or something."

That was the stupidest thing he'd ever heard. Pru would never pull anything so underhanded or cruel. Plus, she'd told him about her solo mommy plans. Why would she seduce him to try and get pregnant when she already had a plan? He knew better. Knew *her* better.

"I would never think that of you. We had a little too much to drink. We both got caught up in the moment. We're both at fault."

Though secretly, he blamed himself. He should have remembered. He should have protected her.

"So, what now?"

"I wanted a baby." She nodded, back in Practical Pru mode. "And now, well, I'm going to have one. Maybe not the way I planned, but I want this baby, Finn."

He knew that, and he would never try and stop her from getting what she wanted. What kind of friend would he be if he did? A shitty one. And Finn Jamison might be a lot of things, but a shitty friend was not one of them.

"Okay."

In a way, it was sort of cool how he'd helped her achieve her dream. Not everyone would understand it, but people could go screw themselves. Pru wanted something and, in a roundabout way, he'd helped make it happen. Wasn't that what friends were supposed to do?

Friends don't knock each other up just because one of them wants a baby.

Well some friends do, apparently.

"Okay?"

He shrugged. "Yeah, I mean, this is what you wanted, right? A baby?" She nodded. "Then I'm really happy for you, Pru."

"You are?"

"Yeah."

The shock of the situation still had him reeling, but he absolutely loved the smile brightening her face. She was happy, more so than he'd ever seen her. How could he be upset by that?

Still, her happiness wasn't the only thing to think about here.

"Do you, ah, do you want me involved?"

Her smile stilted, confusion filling her features. "Do you want to be involved?"

"I…don't know."

He'd never imagined himself as a father. He loved being an uncle. His nieces and nephews were great, but the greatest thing about them was spoiling them rotten, then handing them back to their parents.

Parents. He was going to be someone's father.

Did he want to be a father? He kind of was one, regardless. The baby inside Pru held half of his DNA. That made him a father, but it didn't make him a dad. Everyone had a father, a biological donor, but it took time and caring to be a dad. Help with homework, playing catch in the backyard, advice on dealing with bullies and puberty. That's what a dad did. It's what his had done.

Could he do that knowing it could all be taken away in the blink of an eye? One bad fire, one unsteady building, one bad rescue and he'd be leaving a child who depended on him.

No one is guaranteed tomorrow.

Oh great, and now his dad's favorite phrase rang in his head. Not even a father yet and he was already turning into his old man.

But the more important question was, did Pru want him to be involved? She started this journey with the specific desire to go solo.

"Do *you* want me to be involved?"

Dark brown eyes stared at him, a million questions he couldn't decipher running through her gaze.

"Right now?" She shook her head. "I have no idea what I want besides this baby."

Her hands moved over her abdomen, and his gaze followed. There was a baby in there. *Their* baby. It was weird and scary and amazingly awesome all at the same time.

So much for sex not changing anything.

"I have an appointment in a few weeks to hear the heartbeat and have an ultrasound."

"An ultrasound? Is everything okay?"

She smiled at his slight panic. "Yes. That's just what they do at the first appointment. To check everything out and make sure things are where they're supposed to be and growing properly."

"Oh, cool." He was going to have to hit the web and look up some baby stuff tonight. "Do you want me to go with you?"

"Do you want to go with me?"

They were stuck in a loop. Neither knowing what they wanted, both trying to think of the other. It's why their friendship worked so well, but it made for hard times picking dinner plans.

Or baby decisions, evidently.

"Yeah. I mean, if that's okay with you. I'd like to go and... be supportive and stuff."

She chuckled at his use of the word *stuff*. Excuse him, but this was new territory and he wasn't familiar with all the nomenclature.

"Okay. That'd be nice to have you there for all the support and *stuff*."

"Oh, shut up."

"Hey! You can't be mean to me. I'm pregnant."

"Oh God, you're going to use that excuse for the next nine months, aren't you?"

She grinned. "Yup."

"Then I take back my supportive statement."

She grabbed a couch cushion and flung it at his head. He dodged it, wrapping an arm around her shoulder and tugging her into his side. He ruffled her hair, which she immediately complained about before settling against him.

"Seriously, Pru. I know this is all weird and not how you planned it, but if you're happy, that's all that matters."

"I'm happy, Finn. Really, really happy."

He flicked on the TV, cueing up their favorite show.

"Then I'm happy."

He pasted on a bright smile, but inside, his mind was screaming. His palms sweating with the life-changing news that had just been dropped in his lap, heart beating so loudly he was afraid Pru could hear it. Bruiser stared at him with her dark, puppy-dog eyes, head tilted in a question. He reached out to pat his intuitive dog on her furry head, hiding his fingers in her fur when he noticed them trembling.

He was happy for Pru. She was getting what she wanted, and though he was glad he could help, it meant he was also getting something he never wanted. A child whose world he could possible destroy.

So yeah, he was happy for her, but he was also scared as hell.

Chapter Eight

"Pru." Lilly pushed her glasses up her nose, staring at the file in her hands. "Did you send the deposit check for the Miranda-Snow wedding?"

"Hey!" Mo snatched the file from Lilly's hands. "No more work. We're three feet from home. We agreed to stop taking work home."

"Home is one flight of stairs up." Lilly made a grab for the file, but Mo was quick and shoved it behind her back.

Pru laughed softly. About all the energy she had in her at the moment. Who knew this baby-growing thing would be so exhausting? She was only about a month along, but every day her body felt like she'd run a 5k. And without the benefit of multiple cups of coffee, she had to admit, she was struggling.

Worth it.

Yes, it was all worth it. The lack of energy, the nausea, all of it. She'd endure whatever she had to because it meant she would soon hold her sweet baby in her arms. Arms that at the moment literally ached. Partly from tiredness, but mostly from the desire to be filled with a loving soul who needed her, a person whose whole world depended on her.

Lilly held out a firm hand. "Give that back, Moira. Right now!"

Mo bobbed her eyebrows. "Oooh, whaddaya gonna do if I don't?"

As entertaining as it could be to watch Mo push Lilly's buttons, Pru didn't have the energy for it tonight.

"Mo, give her back the file, and Lilly, yes I handled the deposit, but Mo is right. We did agree to leave work downstairs."

Mo handed back the folder, aiming a bright smile Pru's way.

"What?"

Her friend shrugged. "Nothing. I was just thinking you should thank us."

Reaching their front door, Pru dug her keys out of her purse, inserting the metal apartment key into the lock as she spoke over her shoulder. "For what?"

"For all the years of practice we've given you. Just think of all the fights you've settled between Lil and me."

"We don't fight," Lilly said with a frown. "We disagree."

Mo rolled her eyes, sharing a smile with Pru. "You're going to rock motherhood."

She found the energy for an actual laugh at that true statement, but the moment she opened their apartment door, she heard a noise that caused her laughter to die. Someone was in their apartment. A loud *thud* and some muffled cursing came from the back of the hallway. One of the bedrooms.

Were they being robbed?

Heart in her throat, she turned to her roommates. Mo's face had gone pale as a ghost, Lilly had her cell in her hand, fingers already dialing for the authorities, Pru assumed. As quietly as she could—she didn't want to alert any bad guys to their presence, she'd seen her fair share of crime shows, that was how a B&E turned into a homicide—she started to back away from the door when a familiar voice shouted a very creative curse.

"Wait…Finn?"

"Why are there no words to go with these stupid instructions!" the voice bellowed down the hallway to the open front door.

Yup. She knew that voice. That was definitely her best friend.

"Finn?" she called louder into the apartment. She was pretty sure it was him, but she wasn't stupid. She hovered in the apartment hallway with her roommates, ready to run if her ears were playing tricks on her.

"Pru?" Finn's voice called back to her.

"Oh for the love of—" Lilly shoved her phone back into the pocket of her black slacks. "Pru, what is Finn doing here?"

She shrugged, as clueless as the rest of them. "How should I know?"

"He is your best friend," Mo said. "And the father of your unborn child."

She scowled at Mo. Yeah, but he never came over without informing her, and though they had keys to each other's places for emergencies, he'd never used his before.

She entered the apartment and marched down the hallway to discover Finn in her bedroom surrounded by…

"What is all this?"

A large, empty cardboard box lay on her bed displaying the picture of a beautiful crib with a happy baby smiling in the middle of the perfectly put together furniture. The contents of her bedroom looked nothing like the picture on the box.

Pieces of wood and screws were strewn about the floor. A screwdriver stuck out of Finn's back pocket as he crouched over a large white piece of paper with some sort of building instructions printed on it. And then there was Finn, looking stressed and worried, like a kid who got his hand caught in the cookie jar ten minutes before a nice healthy dinner.

He grimaced, lifting one shoulder. "Surprise?"

"Finn, what are you doing?"

He stood, paper still clutched in his hands as he faced her. "Um, I bought you this crib. I mean, I bought it for the baby. I bought the baby a crib. It was on sale, and I saw it and just... I don't know. I wanted to put it together while you were at work and surprise you with it, but the instructions don't have any words, just pictures, and I can't make out what half of these damn doodles mean."

She shook her head, the tiredness weighing down her limbs replaced with vibrating annoyance. Heat rose on her face as she took in the situation. His heart was in the right place, she knew that, but sometimes Finn overstepped his bounds.

"I never asked you to buy a crib."

His brow rose. Okay, maybe she said that a tad bit harshly, but she was exhausted and didn't have the energy for this right now.

"I know. I wanted to buy it. To surprise you."

Tears threatened, but she willed them back. Damn pregnancy hormones. "Look, Finn. I know you like taking care of people and all, but this is my thing. This baby..." She placed a hand over her stomach, watching as his wary gaze followed her movement. "I've planned for this baby. It may not have happened the way I wanted to begin with, but everything from here on out I have a plan for, a system. It's too soon to buy a crib."

The first trimester was the most dangerous. So many things could go wrong. She'd only told her roommates and Finn about the baby. She didn't plan on telling anyone else for at least another two months. And shopping for anything was out of the question until *after* the first appointment.

When she could have a solid confirmation that things were going well.

She. Had. A. Plan.

"I just wanted to help," he said, voice unsteady as he glanced around the room.

"I don't need any help." This wasn't how it was supposed to happen. This was her baby. *Mine.*

Mo's hand reached out. "Pru, sweetie—"

She brushed off her friend's touch. A storm of emotions churned inside her. She had to leave now, before she lost it in front of everyone. What was going on? Why was she feeling this sudden panic, this fear? A ringing filled her ears, bile rising in her throat. Pushing past the worried faces of her roommates, she ran to the bathroom, slamming the door and crouching by the toilet as the tears flowed.

What was wrong with her? All Finn had been trying to do was something nice for her, for the baby. Why did she turn into such a raging bitch and go off on him like that?

• • •

Finn started to go after Pru, but Lilly stepped forward, holding up a hand.

"I think she needs a minute," the tall, poised woman said with a soft, understanding smile. "I'll go stand outside the door in case she needs anything."

He wanted to refuse her, wanted to run after Pru and make sure she was okay, but he knew Lilly was probably right. The woman usually was. So he nodded.

Once she left, he glanced around the room. Looking at his supposed surprise with fresh eyes. Of course Pru was mad. She hated surprises. He knew that.

He'd just been at such a loss over what to do, he'd acted without thinking. Gone and bought a damn crib thinking it would somehow help this weird situation they found themselves in.

"Don't beat yourself up too much." Mo spoke gently.

He glanced up to see the short woman smiling at him.

"I screwed up."

She nodded. "Yeah, but you were trying to be sweet. That's gotta count for something."

He sure as hell hoped so, but… "I just wanted to help. To do something to make this easier on her, and I failed." He kicked the abandoned pile of crib parts next to his foot, tossing the useless directions on top of the wood. "I can't even put together a stupid baby crib. How am I going to…"

But he couldn't finish the question because he didn't even know what he was seeking answers to.

"What?" Mo asked. "Be a dad?"

Yes. No. He didn't want to be a dad. Pru didn't want him to be the dad. She wanted to do this on her own, and he was fine with that. How could he be a good father when he couldn't even put a goddamn crib together?

"I'm not trying to be a dad. Pru doesn't want that." He didn't want that. "I just want…to contribute in some way. To help."

And maybe to alleviate some of the crushing sense of responsibility His mom and dad had told him time and time again that if he ever got a girl pregnant, they expected him to participate fully as a parent, but that wasn't what Pru wanted. Years of conditioning and his own damn conscience warred with the wishes of his best friend, and he didn't know how to make it all stop.

Mo laughed, blond and pink curls bouncing. "You've been friends with Pru for how many years now? You know she doesn't easily accept help of any kind."

Yeah, he knew.

"So are you really doing this for her?" Mo tilted her head.

"Or is this for you?"

What the hell did that mean? Of course he was doing this for Pru. What did he have to gain from spending hours staring at stupid scribbles that made no sense and cursing at a pile of inanimate wood? This was to help Pru. Nothing more.

"You two got yourselves into a very strange situation here, Finn." Mo shook her head, stepping closer. "I'm not gonna lie. Even I could never imagine a situation like this. But it's here. It's happening, and I think you both need to sit down and have a real conversation about it all."

"Pru and I are fine." He ran his hands through the hair on the top of his head. "She's just freaking out because of baby hormones or something."

Mo arched a brow, and shame immediately filled him. Okay, that was a stupid thing to say, but he was so far out of his element here he didn't even know which way was up anymore.

"Sorry. I didn't mean that. You're right. I should have known better. Pru doesn't like help. I shouldn't have bought the stupid crib." He started to gather the pieces of wood and screws, tossing them into the box on the bed. "I'll just—"

Mo's gentle hand on his arm paused his frantic movements.

"Finn, it was a sweet gesture, and I know this situation is hard on you, too, but just remember to be open and honest with her. Okay? Everything will work out in the end."

His rapid heartbeat slowed with the optimistic woman's words. He let out a small chuckle, slowing but continuing to gather the bits and pieces of the failed crib. "Thanks, Mo. But I don't think this situation is going to turn into the happily ever after you have in mind." Over the years he'd come to find Mo was an eternal romantic. It was cute. Kind of naive, but cute. "Pru and I will be fine, I'm sure. But we're just friends."

The small woman patted his arm. "Keep telling yourself that, big guy. The harder the fight, the sweeter the fall."

She gave him a quick hug before heading out of the room. He continued to pick up, packing everything into the box as he ignored Mo's denial. He and Pru were friends. Nothing more. Just because they'd had sex once and she'd gotten pregnant didn't mean their friendship had to change. He didn't want to be a dad, and she wasn't asking him to be one. Win win. Right? So he made one tiny little mistake. From now on he'd ask her what she needed for the baby before going ahead and getting it.

Problem solved.

For now, he'd give her space while he regrouped. Get this firewood masquerading as a crib the hell out of here and send her some apology chili cheese fries. Could you get chili cheese fries delivered? He didn't know, but he was going to find out. Because this failed attempt at…whatever the hell he'd been trying to do just proved that fatherhood wasn't in the cards for him. He'd let Pru handle baby stuff from now on.

Everything would be fine, no matter what the sick, tightening cramp in his stomach told him. Things would be okay. They had to be.

Chapter Nine

F: *You up?*

P: *It's 2 in the afternoon and you are not as funny as you think, Jamison.*

Finn chuckled as he read the reply from Pru. Happy she got his intended joke when he texted her the universal booty call. Honestly, he'd been a little worried. Things had been off with them ever since his dumb ass had decided to surprise Pru with the baby crib. The mess of wood and screws now lay in the workout room at the station, a taunting reminder of his failure, and of why he needed to step back and let Pru take the lead on this.

This was her thing, her dream. Just because he happened to help in the process didn't mean she expected him to continue helping. He just didn't know what to do, how to step up or step back. He knew Pru didn't need his help, but how did he shut off the voice inside his head demanding he do his share?

He tapped Pru's picture at the top of the conversation, hit the phone icon, then pressed the cell to his ear. He'd sent Pru an apology text after leaving her apartment the night before, but he'd only gotten a brief reply. Now, the phone rang twice. He held his breath, wondering if she would pick up.

"Oh my God, why are you calling me? Why can't you text like a normal millennial?"

He laughed, the tension in his chest easing as Pru's grumpy voice filled the line. Pru *hated* talking on the phone. She actively avoided it, making Mo and Lilly field all their business calls. If she cared enough to answer, she couldn't be that upset.

"We were texting, but my fingers were cramping. Besides, I wanted to call and apologize again."

A soft sigh filtered over the line. "You don't have to apologize. In fact, I was just going to call you."

A small weight lifted from his tense shoulders at her words. He hated conflict. Having Pru angry with him gave him a sour stomach no amount of antacid could cure.

"You were?"

"Yes, I know you were just trying to help, even though I don't need any."

He chuckled at her insistence. Pru could be stuck on the side of I-25 with no gas and a five mile walk to the nearest gas station and still not admit to needing help.

"But it was very sweet of you, and I'm sorry I acted..."

"Like a reality TV star getting voted off the island?"

"I was going to say 'a bit hormonal.'"

"Hey!" He winced when his sharp exclamation woke Bruiser, who'd been sleeping peacefully in his lap. He rubbed the tiny dog behind her ears, lulling her back to sleep. "If I had said that, I'd be in trouble. How come you can say it?"

"Men should never call women hormonal. Even when they are," she explained.

"Double standard."

"Yeah? Once women get paid the same as men for doing twice the work, then we can talk about double standards."

She had a solid point. "Touché."

Glad they seemed to be back to normal, or as normal as they could get for the time being, he asked, "You wanna come over later? We've got two episodes of *Single Woman Looking* to finish."

"Tonight?"

"Yeah. Is that a problem?"

"Yes, it's a problem, Finn. A big problem."

"Why?" He'd apologized, she'd apologized. He thought they were good now.

"Oh, man." Mocking laughter filled his ear. "You totally forgot."

"Forgot? Forgot what?"

"About tonight."

Tonight? Did they have plans? He didn't remember making any. He glanced down at Bruiser, who stirred in his lap. The pup glanced up and cocked her head as if to say *I'm your dog, not your social secretary.* Okay, so no help from Bru.

"Oooooo, you are in so much trouble."

The relentless giggling, he could do without. She was having far too much fun at his expense.

"Okay, I give. What did I forget?"

She hummed before answering. "I don't know if I should tell you and save your ass or let you crash and burn."

"Save my ass please. You like my ass. You told me so."

The evil laughter on the other end of the phone died. Oops, was he not supposed to bring up things like that? It wasn't like they could pretend sleeping together never happened. Not anymore. Not with the evidence of it rapidly growing inside Pru's womb.

"Your ass is okay," she finally replied. "I suppose you could say I like it, but it's not as great as my magnificent breasts."

Oh, so they were going to play it like that? Okay, he could joke. But not about her breasts, because she was right—they were magnificent.

"No argument from me on that one. Boobs beat butt any day of the week."

She snorted. "You're such a guy."

"Guilty."

"Anyway, much as I'd love to see you get what's coming to you for forgetting, she would be devastated if you didn't show up, so I'm going to remind you tonight is your—"

"Mom's birthday dinner."

"Bingo!"

Shit. He had forgotten. In his defense, his mother's actual birthday was in two weeks, but she was going on a cruise with his father so they were having the family celebration early.

"At least tell me you got her a present?"

"Of course, I did." He wasn't a horrible son, just slightly forgetful. "I bought her that painting of the front range she had her eye on at the People's Fair this summer."

His mother, a retired English teacher, loved collecting local artists' works. Made gift shopping a breeze.

"She's going to love that. I got her some opal earrings from the rock shop up in Estes Park."

And his mother would love those, too, because she loved Pru. Having four sons, his mom always doted on Pru whenever Finn brought her over. Which had been many times throughout the years. She liked to comment that Pru was the daughter she always wanted and never had. And now Pru would give his mother another grandchild.

Wait—did Pru want his parents to know? Another thing they needed to talk about. The list was ever growing.

"You wanna ride with me?" Because even though it was a family dinner, Pru was considered family and therefore invited. "No need for both of us to drive out to Lakewood."

Not that it was far from the city, twenty minutes or so, but why waste the gas if they were both going to the same place?

"Um, sure. Makes sense." She hesitated for a moment before speaking again. "Do we tell them about the baby?"

The churning in his gut was back. At this point, he might as well invest in an antacid company. He imagined he'd be buying it by the bucket load for the next nine months.

"Maybe not right now." He hurried to add, "Unless you want to?"

Pru's heavy sigh filled his ear. "No. I mean, yes, eventually we need to tell them. I want to tell them. I think. But maybe not tonight. Tonight is about celebrating your mom, and I don't want to…share this with her until we know a little more. Plus, I'm still in the first trimester. They say to wait until the second in case… Well, anyway. Let's wait a bit longer."

Seemed logical to him. And it gave him a pass on explaining to his parents how he'd knocked up his best friend but wouldn't be assuming the role of daddy, something he knew would disappoint them both greatly. His parents loved their sons, but they would expect Finn to care for his baby as a full-time parent would. How was he going to tell them Pru didn't want that, and he didn't want that? It was a very unique and weird situation that required a plan of action. Good thing he had the queen of planning on his side.

"I'll pick you up around five?" he asked.

"Sounds good."

"Later."

"Bye." He started to hang up when her voice made him pause. "And give Bruiser two treats for me."

He hung up with a huge grin on his face. He glanced down to his pup.

"Well, Bru Baby, Pru said you need treats."

At the word "treats," two floppy ears perked up. Bruiser abandoned her beloved chew toy and ran to the kitchen, nails scraping on the hardwood floor as she careened into the cabinets.

"Ouch. Slow down, girl."

Bruiser never slowed down. When she wanted something, she raced for it, full steam. Kind of like another beautiful female he knew. They both made him smile.

• • •

Pru clutched the tiny wrapped package in her hands, sliding into the passenger seat of Finn's car.

"Where's Bruiser?" His mother loved the little furball as much as Finn did. He usually took her along whenever he went to his parents' house.

"Jordan's home from fall break."

Ah, that explained it. Finn's younger brother was allergic to pet dander. It was why they never had any pets growing up, even though she knew Mrs. Jamison loved animals. At least she got to live her pup-loving dreams through Finn like Pru did.

"So how is he doing at Pepperdine?"

They chatted about Finn's little brother and his first year away from home. So far, he was the first Jamison to go to college out of state. They were a tight-knit family, oddly so, like one of those from the 1950s TV shows Aunt Rose used to watch on the late-night rerun channel.

They pulled up to Finn's childhood home, a pretty blue two-story with one large pine tree out front and two huge bushes that bloomed with the sweetest smelling lilacs in early May. Finn turned off the car, hopping out to come around to her side and open her door. It wasn't unusual. He always opened her door for her—or anyone who rode with him—good manners instilled by his parents. But for some reason, the gesture made her feel strange. Didn't matter that she'd done this with Finn a hundred times before. This time was different. She was going to a family dinner with a man she'd slept with. A man whose baby she was having.

"You okay?" he asked when she didn't get out of the car.

"Yeah, of course." She was being silly. So what if she slept with Finn and was having his kid? It wasn't like he'd told his parents or anything. They wouldn't know that she was arriving at this dinner with carnal knowledge of their son.

Oh God, she had to stop thinking about it. Why couldn't she stop thinking about it?

Because he's standing there with his handsome face and sexy tattoos and beautiful eyes and now that I've had him, I can't stop replaying that night in my mind.

Stupid, sexy best friend.

And she had the result of their one night together currently growing inside her. Crap! What if his mother could tell? Flipping down the visor, she glanced in the tiny mirror. Was she glowing? She heard pregnant women glowed. Did Mrs. Jamison have that grandmother sixth sense? Would she be able to look at Pru and know she was carrying her grandchild?

"Pru." Finn's soothing voice cut through her fog of panic. "Everything will be fine. They won't know anything we don't tell them."

She glanced over to him. His expression looked calm enough, but his eyes gave him away. The same tight panic she felt in her chest echoed in his bright blue gaze.

"You sure about that?"

He swallowed, rubbing his hands over his face before glancing at his parents' house. "Yeah. We just act normal, focus on my mom, and everything will be fine. Later, when we've figured more stuff out, we'll tell them. Everything will be fine then, too."

Maybe if they both said it enough times, they'd start to believe it.

She got out as Finn grabbed his mother's present from the back seat.

"Finn, Pru, you made it!"

Pru felt the smile curl her lips as she glanced up to see Mrs. Jamison standing in the doorway of the house, grey hair pulled back into a bun like always, a big welcoming smile lighting up her face. Wendy Jamison had been a second mother to Pru.

"Wouldn't miss it, Mom." Finn moved up the front porch steps and placed a kiss on his mother's cheek. "Happy birthday."

"Thank you, dear. And you"—Wendy held her arms out—"get over here."

Pru happily stepped into the loving embrace. "Happy birthday, Wendy."

"Well, come on. Everyone is already here, and the grandkids are *starving*. Or so they keep telling me."

Right... Pru would bet their grandmother had been sneaking them cookies behind their parents' backs all night. *The perks of being a grandma*, Wendy always told her with a wink.

They sat at the table, exchanging hellos with everyone as they settled. No one mentioned whether she looked any different or acted like anything was off between her and Finn. Perhaps they could pull this off. For a little while. Once she started to show, they'd have to tell Finn's family. She didn't want to keep it a secret from them, anyway.

A small spark of joy burned deep in her chest as she realized her baby would be getting a family beyond her—grandparents, aunts and uncles, cousins.

A family.

Her eyes misted over with the knowledge. Damn hormones! She couldn't cry. Not now, everyone would know something was up. Blinking back the tears, she grabbed the dish of mashed potatoes Finn's niece handed her.

"So Pru," Wendy said as they all dug into the delicious dinner. "Tell me what's new in your life? Any handsome men you're seeing?"

Finn choked on the sip of water he'd just taken. She squeezed his leg, trying to silently tell him to keep his cool, but it had the opposite effect. He gasped, his sputtering increasing. Jordan, who sat on his other side, started patting Finn's back as he cleared the liquid from his throat.

"Finn, dear." Wendy held a hand to her chest as she stared with concern and confusion at her son. "Are you all right?"

Crap! She had to deflect so Wendy didn't start to suspect anything from Finn's panic.

"Am I dating? No, sadly the men in Denver are...lacking."

Wendy's gaze came back to her, and the woman chuckled at her statement. Finn, however, didn't seem to find it as amusing. His eyes narrowed, but she ignored his glare and asked his mother about her upcoming cruise.

The rest of the evening went by nicely. Wendy loved her gifts and sent everyone home with an extra birthday cupcake.

Once they were in the car and on the road back into the city, Finn glanced toward Pru.

"Lacking, Pru? Seriously?"

She chuckled. "Well, what did you want me to say? 'Oh, yes, Mrs. Jamison, I had a lovely time the other night doing the naked tango with your son. Oh, and by the way, I'm now carrying his unborn child. Surprise!'"

He gave a defeated sigh. "No. I guess you couldn't say that. Unless we wanted to spend the rest of the night explaining in detail how this all happened."

Not too much detail, she hoped. She couldn't imagine a mother wanted to know the exact details of how her son knocked up his best friend.

And now it was in her head again. Every delicious moment, every exquisite detail. Finn's rough hands touching her so softly, the contrast driving her wild. Her body started to heat with the memory of what he could do with those hands, his tongue, his—

Whoa!

She needed to stop thinking about that night. They weren't going there again. Things were weird enough as it was.

The rest of the ride was silent except for the soft music filtering in from the car's speakers. Finally, they arrived at her apartment. She'd never been so glad to be home, which was strange and a little sad. She loved hanging out with Finn and his family, but tonight had been stressful. She hated keeping secrets, especially from someone as sweet as Wendy Jamison.

"Thanks for the ride."

"Thanks for coming. I know Mom loves seeing you."

"Your mom's the best."

He smiled. "I agree."

She smiled back, and there was a moment, a single second when she could have sworn she saw something in his gaze—heat. A heat she remembered.

The last time she'd seen it in his eyes, she'd ended up pregnant.

She found herself swaying forward, toward him. His gaze flitted down to her mouth, which opened of its own accord, her tongue coming out to graze her suddenly parched lips.

He was going to kiss her again. She knew it. She could feel it.

But then, he shifted back against the seat, head turning to face the windshield. His fingers gripped the steering wheel tightly.

"Night, Pru."

Shaking herself out of whatever stupor had fuzzed her brain, she opened the car door. "Good night, Finn."

She hurried to the front door of her building, practically running. What the hell had that been? They'd almost kissed. Again! Maybe it was just baby hormones. Yes, that was all. They just had some weirdness going on right now because of this odd situation.

This would all blow over soon. Things would get back to normal again.

Except there was this tiny doubtful voice whispering in the back of her mind, causing her to tense with the fearful knowledge that one night with Finn hadn't been enough to sate her. Why did her body crave what her mind knew was a bad idea? And was she strong enough to deny herself?

Chapter Ten

Pru woke up clutching the oddly long U-shaped pillow Finn had delivered to her place a week and a half ago after she complained about her back hurting like she was an eighty-year-old who'd worked hauling bricks her entire life. He had offered to find a solution for her, and the next morning he'd shown up with the heavenly cushion, saying it was the same kind that his sister-in-law swore saved her back during her last two pregnancies. He texted every day, checking in with her, seeing if she needed anything, dropping by at random times to give her pillows and morning sickness lollipops. Which she very much appreciated, since the term "morning sickness" was a big fat lie. More like "any time of the day or night sickness" and especially when Lilly drank her disgusting-smelling spinach and mango smoothies after working out.

Finn had gone into caring overdrive. Though he'd stop purchasing anything for the baby since the disastrous crib incident, he said taking care of her was just what a best friend was supposed to do. Since every day she felt crappier and crappier, she had no problem with him pampering her. As long as he didn't try to take baby decision out of her hands again, they were good.

She laughed at herself, the chuckle turning into a groan when her stomach pitched and rolled.

"Oh, come on, Peanut." She rubbed her flat belly. "Mommy hasn't even gotten out of bed yet. Can we hold off on the hurling for five minutes?"

The acid working its way up her throat said no, no they could not. She tossed back her blankets and raced for the bathroom. Luckily, their apartment had two, and the moment she started puking twice a day, Lilly and Mo insisted she take the front bathroom while they shared the back. She made it just in time to heave up…nothing, mostly, but some water and the remnants of the late-night ice cream binge she'd snuck when she woke up at midnight craving rocky road.

"This baby-making is hard work."

She clung to the toilet bowl, letting her stomach settle before she flushed and stood to thoroughly brush her teeth. A soft tap sounded on the door.

"Yes?"

"I come bearing special candy." Mo's voice filtered through the closed door.

Feeling slightly better after her new morning puking ritual, Pru turned the knob, opening the bathroom door a crack.

"You better mean my nausea lollipops and not the *special candy* in the goody bags from the 'Marriage of Mary and Jane' we did last spring."

The two brides thought it would be hilarious to combine their love of a certain plant now legal in Colorado and the fact that their first names were slang for said plant. Since their wedding had been twenty-one and over only, they'd given each guest a goody bag with a sample of Colorado's newest economy-driver with the strict instruction that the contents could not leave the state.

"Hey, I might have been raised by a couple of hippies, but even I know you don't give a pregnant woman weed." Mo lifted the small bag Finn dropped off last week. "Lollys to the rescue. And you really need to keep these by your bed for the mornings."

She should, but she kept forgetting. "Thanks, Mo."

"You're welcome. Oh, and Lilly already made her smoothie and promises to finish it while you shower so the smell doesn't bother you."

Bless her understanding and thoughtful roommates.

"Want me to make you some toast?"

She moaned. "Yes please. I don't deserve you two. You're too good to me."

"You deserve the best, Pru, because you are the best."

Mo blew her a kiss, avoiding stepping any closer to the bathroom and the lovely smell of vomit wafting in the air.

"Here." Mo handed over one sucker. "I'll put the rest in your nightstand."

"Thank you."

"Welcome. Oh, and Lilly wants to have a meeting to check in on how the Franks-Sharma wedding is going."

"Okay, I'll be out in a few."

They only had a few weddings left this year. The fall frenzy had tapered off, and the winter season was never very busy. A few Holiday Wonderland themes here and there, but most of the Colorado snowy weddings were destination affairs held at the ski resorts. They'd worked with a few in the past, but a lot of the resorts had their own wedding coordinators.

That was fine. There was plenty of wedded bliss to go around, and they tended to handle clientele on a slightly smaller budget than the big, fancy resort weddings allowed. Pru could handle large sums of money, but the type of service the six-digit brides and grooms required wasn't quite what

Mile High Happiness provided.

She brought the lollipop into the shower with her, scrubbing her hair and body all while sucking whatever miracle ingredients were in that semi-delicious candy that settled her stomach. Once she'd finished, dried off, and gotten dressed, she went to the kitchen to see her toast waiting with a note indicating the others had gone into the office and she should meet them there.

Now that her stomach was settled, her appetite returned with vigor. She practically inhaled the first piece of toast, grabbing the second to munch on her ride down on the elevator to their office on the first floor.

"Good morning," she called to her friends and business partners as she pushed through the flower-etched glass door of their office.

"Feeling better?" Mo asked, sitting in one of the plush chairs they had for clients.

"Much, thank you."

"I made some peppermint tea for you."

Lilly nodded to a mug on the desk in front of her. Steam and the pungent aroma of mint rose from the cup, hitting Pru's nostrils and settling her stomach even more.

Seriously. Best. Friends. *Ever.*

"Thanks."

"We received a request from a couple who wants to have a February wedding at Union Station."

"February?" That was four months away. "That's cutting it close."

They normally required six months of lead-time on a wedding before they accepted.

"I know," Lilly said, shuffling some papers in front of her. "But they're willing to pay extra for the rush."

Pru noticed the slight tightening of her friend's fingers. She put down the tea she'd just picked up and placed a hand over Lilly's. "Lil, we're doing fine. We don't need to take every job that comes our way anymore. I do the books, remember? We're in the black."

Green eyes gazed up from behind black-rimmed glasses. "I know. I just…"

She just felt guilty for the thing that happened five years ago. The thing they never spoke of. The thing that almost ruined their business. *Almost,* but not quite. Lilly still blamed herself even if Pru and Mo didn't.

"Let's see what they want," Mo said with a smile. "Maybe it won't be too hard. We're in our slow season, and everyone deserves their dream wedding."

Lilly gave them both a grateful smile, and Pru realized she wasn't the only lucky one in this friendship. They might gripe and snap at each other from time to time, but she loved these women and they loved her. They all came together to support one another, no matter what struggles they were facing.

And speaking of struggles…

"I'm in, but I need to leave after lunch. Finn's picking me up for my appointment."

Her friends grinned.

"Finn's taking you?" Mo asked.

"Yeah, he, um, wanted to come."

"Good." Lilly nodded. "He should be pulling his own weight in this."

"I don't need his help. I just don't want to block him out if he wants to be involved."

"Sounds reasonable. I think you should involve him."

"I think you should jump him again."

"Mo!" Her cheeks heated. "We're friends."

The chipper woman snorted. "Friends who had sex and are now having a baby together. The barn door's open, Prudence. The cow's already out. Enjoy the milk!"

"I don't even know what that means."

Lilly pushed her glasses up her nose, staring at her papers. "Something about sex, I imagine."

No way. She wasn't going there again. Look what happened the first time.

Sure, it'd been the most amazing sex of her life, but they were having a kid. *She* was having a kid. She was having his kid… Whatever, it was complicated, and sex would only complicate it further. They could absolutely not fall back into bed together. No matter how many hot dreams she'd had since that night.

Nope.

She wouldn't do it.

Not again.

They worked all through the morning and into lunch. Mo ran out to pick up sandwiches and another bag of anti-nausea lollipops, for which Pru was eternally grateful. Though she still insisted they didn't need to cover it for financial reasons, they all agreed to accept the February rush wedding.

Before she knew it, there was a knock on their office door, and Finn's head popped in.

"Ladies."

"Oh, hey, Daddy."

Finn's smile fell, looking like he tried to keep it but just ended up with an awkward grimace.

Pru elbowed Mo.

"What? Are we not joking about this yet?"

How Moira could laugh off everything in life was beyond her. The woman could see sunshine in a hurricane.

"You ready to go?" he asked, smile now completely gone.

"Yeah. I'm ready." She gathered her jacket and purse. "See you in about an hour or so," she called to the other women, following Finn out the door and into the parking lot.

He opened the car door for her, and she shook her head

with a smile. "What? No bike?"

"You're pregnant, Pru. You can't ride a motorcycle."

Only because she didn't know how to drive one. But if she did, she assumed it would be perfectly acceptable to ride one until her belly got too big. She didn't actually know. It wasn't one of the areas she researched.

They drove the ten minutes to her doctor's office and sat in the waiting room. It was filled with a variety of women and some men, looking everything from excited to bored to terrified. Finn sat by her side, holding her hand in comfort, but his leg nervously bounced up and down, jiggling their chairs with the frantic motion.

At least she wasn't the only one freaking out a little. Hopefully after today's appointment, things would be clearer for them.

"Prudence C.? The doctor will see you now."

She rose from her seat, Finn standing with her. The nurse led them back, taking her weight, a urine sample, and her blood pressure and then instructing her to disrobe and put on a paper gown before she left the room.

"All right, turn around."

One dark blond eyebrow rose. "Seriously?"

"Yes."

"It's not like I've forgotten what you look like naked. You can make me turn around all you want, but that image is branded into my—"

She smashed a hand over his mouth, her cheeks warmed, and a small giggle escaped her lips. "Shut up, you perv. Just because you've seen it once doesn't give you a free pass for all future viewings."

Something wet and smooth caressed her palm. She quickly pulled her hand away. "Ew! Did you just lick my hand?"

He chuckled. The stupid, sexy jerk.

"Just reminding you what else this tongue has touched."

Was he seriously flirting with her now? Here? And if he was, why was she enjoying it so much?

"Finn!"

"Okay, okay. I'll turn around. But it seems weird."

"This whole situation is weird," she grumbled as she started to shimmy out of her clothes the moment his back was turned.

Once she'd settled on the cold, crinkly paper on top of the exam table, paper gown securely covering all the important bits, she cleared her throat. "You can turn around now."

Finn turned, his teasing smile going soft. His hand reached out to grasp hers. "Hey, you know everything's going to be okay. Right?"

She didn't know that, but she hoped. Hoped that, somehow, they could navigate this tricky situation they'd gotten themselves into. Hoped that she could still have what she wanted without taking anything away from her best friend. Hoped that she'd still be able to fit into her favorite pair of jeans after she popped this kid out.

A soft tap on the door prevented her from answering.

"Hello," Dr. Richardson called out as she entered the room. "Hello, Prudence. How are you feeling lately?"

"A little nauseous, but otherwise fine."

"Good, good. And is this the father?" The doctor glanced at Finn.

"Yeah, um, yes, this is my…this is Finn."

"A pleasure to meet you, Finn."

Finn stuck out his free hand, accepting the shake her doctor offered. "Nice to meet you, too."

"Okay, let's get started and get a look at your baby. What do you say?"

She said *ahhhhhhhhhhhhh!*

But only in her head. Outside she simply smiled as Dr.

Richardson scrubbed her hands in the sink before donning gloves and instructing her to lie back. Finn stayed near her head, never letting go of her hand as the doctor wheeled over a machine with a video screen and a wand that looked like something Mo might keep in her bedside drawer.

The doctor rolled something that looked suspiciously like a condom onto the wand thing and squirted some liquid over it.

"Okay, this might feel a bit uncomfortable, but it's going to give us a great view of your baby."

She winced in discomfort, but honestly, it wasn't too terrible.

"Okay, you hear that?"

If the doc meant the weird wooshing, whirring sound, then yeah, she heard it, but she had no idea what it meant.

"Oh, well, that's something."

What? What was something? Was there something wrong with her baby? Her pulse raced, a million horrible scenarios running through her mind, her dreams of motherhood crashing around her, wrenching her heart as she cursed herself and her body for being a failure.

She squeezed Finn's hand, grateful when he bent down and kissed her temple, whispering in her ear.

"It's okay, Pru. Everything is fine."

How did he know? He wasn't a doctor!

One large hand held hers, the other stroking her hair, calming her racing heart as the doctor moved the wand thing around. What the woman was looking for, she had no idea. Everything on the screen just looked like a black and white blob to her. How did people know what they were looking for on these things?

"Hmm, let's just take a look and—oh yes, just as I thought."

Dr. Richardson smiled, pointing to the screen. "See,

there's one healthy heartbeat."

Oh, thank heavens. A strong, healthy heartbeat. Everything was fine.

"And there's another healthy heartbeat."

Say what now?

"Congratulations, you two," the doc said with a smile. "It's twins."

Chapter Eleven

Twins? Twins!

The word buzzed in her brain like a bee at a barbeque, consuming her every thought even if she couldn't quite get a grasp on it.

"Twins?" the question whooshed out of her on a choked gasp.

"Yes. The fertility medication I put you on can increase the possibility of releasing multiple eggs, resulting in twins. Remember when we discussed that?"

Somewhere in her muddled brain, she vaguely remembered them discussing that when she started this journey.

"Now," the doctor continued. "Because this is a high-risk pregnancy, we'll need to monitor you more closely—"

"Is something wrong with the babies?"

Her heart pounded, threatening to beat right out of her chest. She gripped Finn's hand tighter, or maybe he clutched hers, she couldn't tell. All she knew was the only thing keeping her from losing her mind right now was the firm grasp he had on her. He anchored her, keeping her in the moment instead of a million miles ahead, worrying about every eventuality that might befall their babies. She might be Practical Pru, but that didn't mean she couldn't overreact when faced with extenuating circumstances.

"Oh no, nothing is wrong, but any pregnancy involving multiples is considered high risk because of the strain on the mother and babies. We simply want to track your progress carefully to make sure everyone is growing healthily. Okay?"

"That sounds great, doc. Thank you."

She nodded along with Finn's words, suddenly extremely grateful he'd asked to come along. She needed someone to lean on right now, while she processed the huge curveball that came after the pile of bricks that was this situation.

"Here's a copy of photos for you two."

She reached out and grabbed the glossy strip of photos from the doctor. Honestly, it still just looked like a black and white blur to her. There were two outlined circled with tiny blobs in them and small typeface claiming *Baby 1* and *Baby 2* above each circle.

"Wow."

She turned her head slightly at Finn's softly uttered exclamation. The left corner of his mouth ticked up in that lopsided smile. He stared at the images as if he could actually see babies. All she saw was her carefully laid plans being blown to hell and back.

Two! Two babies! At the same time. How would she handle this? She hadn't planned for twins.

Hadn't planned on Finn being the father, either, but here we are.

True. She'd rolled with the first surprise; she could damn well roll with the second. All she had to do was adjust her plan, move some numbers around, double her baby shopping list, plan for two of everything instead of one... Yeah, no problem.

Dr. Richardson grabbed the chart again from the counter, pen poised to take notes as she asked, "Now are you having any issues you'd like to talk about today?"

Still reeling from the news and making mental lists to hold back the panic, Pru shook her head, content to get out of there and have her freak-out in private instead of in a doctor's office covered by nothing but a stiff, scratchy paper gown.

"Actually, doctor, she's been having a lot of nausea. And not just in the mornings—it's pretty constant."

She narrowed her eyes, glaring at Finn. He didn't need to take over completely—she could tell the doctor about her own symptoms.

But you didn't because you're having a tiny breakdown, and he knows it because he's your best friend. Your best friend whose TWINS you're carrying.

Could you be a bitch to yourself? Because Pru was pretty sure that was happening right now.

"Nausea is common in pregnancy, even more so with multiples. I can prescribe an anti-nausea medication for you."

"Is that safe for the babies?"

Dr. Richardson smiled at Finn. "Completely safe. We want the mother to keep all those healthy nutrients in her belly so the babies can grow big and strong."

She listened as her doctor and best friend, aka the father of her unborn babies, talked about her pregnancy and symptoms, contributing nothing to the conversation herself.

Get it together, Pru. This was supposed to be your thing. Your journey. Stop freaking out about minor details and take control of the situation.

Finding out she was having twins could hardly be called a *minor detail*, but her inner diva was right. She needed to get her head back in the game and regain her power.

"Thank you, Dr. Richardson. I'd appreciate that."

The doctor wrote something on the pad in her hands and passed the paper to Pru. "This should keep the nausea down to a minimum, but if you find yourself not being able to eat or keep anything down, please call the office right away. We'd need to check you for hyperemesis gravidarum to make sure you're not losing important nutrients for you and the babies."

In her research, she'd come across the condition, but her morning sickness was nowhere near that bad. Good thing, because she could barely handle the news the doc had laid on her today. One crisis at a time, please.

Not that having twins was a crisis in any way. In fact, the thought of two little babies to love and care for made her heart soar. All she'd asked for was one baby, and here she was, being blessed with two.

Stressful? Sure. Amazing? No doubt.

"In the meantime, make sure you're drinking plenty of water, eating a healthy diet, and see Annette on the way out. She'll help you schedule your next few appointments." The older woman nodded to both of them. "Congratulations, Mom and Dad."

With that, Dr. Richardson smiled and exited the room, leaving Pru alone with Finn and the exciting/terrifying news.

• • •

At that moment, a strong breeze could have knocked Finn over. Which was saying something, considering he stayed upright while wielding a fire hose on a regular basis. Those things could spit out pressure of up to 300psi. But, apparently, all it took to shake Finn was two babies who barely weighed a few ounces at this point.

Twins.

He'd been having a bit of a mental freak-out since they arrived at the doctor's office. He'd never imagined himself visiting a place like this, but here he was, to support Pru. But the moment the doctor handed over those glossy, black and white pictures, the freak-out went into full-blown panic. The news of two babies slammed into the last bit of calm he'd been holding on to, threatening to send his carefully constructed demeanor right down the drain.

But something else happened, too. The second he saw those two little blurry images, his chest filled with awe.

I made those.

Or at least helped, anyway.

Bewilderment blocked out everything else for just a moment. Sure, he was still scared shitless and confused as to what the hell they were going to do about this whole situation. But look what they'd done. They'd created two little lives. Two tiny humans who might have Pru's smile and his eyes. Her headstrong attitude and his sense of humor.

He glanced over at Pru, who looked as shocked as he felt. Sympathetic humor tilted his lips as he stared at his poor best friend. She lived by her plans. This must be throwing her for quite the loop. First her idea of solo mommy-hood got waylaid by their night of…exploration. Then she found out it wasn't one baby she'd be expecting, but two.

But like the champ she was, Pru was already working things out. He could see the calculation in her dark brown eyes. She may be panicking, but she was also strategizing. Practical Pru. Nothing could keep her down for long.

"You ready to go?"

"Huh? Oh, yeah."

She slid off the table, gaze unfocused as she started to disrobe. Okaaaay, maybe she wasn't as together as he'd thought. Twenty minutes ago, she just about blew a brain cell at the thought of undressing in front of him. Now she was tossing off the paper gown, mindlessly grabbing for her clothes, as naked as the day she was born, seemingly unaware or uncaring of his presence.

She's not okay.

Her mind might be grinding behind those beautiful eyes, but it wasn't planning. Or it was, but it was also freaking out. Big time. He needed to do something. Help her. And it started with grabbing her discarded clothing and helping her into it without ogling her body like the perv she'd earlier accused him of being.

Even if he was a bit pervy.

He tried his hardest not to look, but he remembered how magnificent Pru was in all her naked glory, and it was hard not to sneak a peek. By the tightening in his pants, that wasn't the only hard thing.

Once she was dressed, he wrapped an arm around her waist and led her out of the exam room, heading to the front desk. Luckily, Pru had enough wherewithal to schedule her next few appointments. Finn made a note in his calendar app to make sure he got his shifts rearranged so he could be there for each one.

He was just being a good friend, making sure he was there if she needed him. That was all.

They left the doctor's office, Pru still allowing him to guide her, which really had him worried. Pru was never this zombie-like.

When they got to his car, he opened her door, helping her sit and pulling the seat belt around her. She allowed all of it. Very not Pru-like. She had to snap out of it.

"Pru?" He gently cupped her face between his hands. "Talk to me."

Her gaze finally focused on him, her brown eyes blinking until recognition lit in their dark depths.

"Twins, Finn. Twins!"

He couldn't stop the small smile from curling his lips. "I know, Precious. But everything will be okay. I promise."

She snorted. "So like a man to promise something you can in no way be sure of delivering."

Ah, there she was. His feisty Pru was back.

"I know. Men, ugh! Right?"

She laughed, lightly pushing his shoulder. "Shut up and let's go."

Fear receding—now that she seemed to be back to her old self—he shut the door and made his way around to the driver's side. He knew he was supposed to bring her straight back to work, but he found himself going left instead of right when they pulled out of the office parking lot.

"Finn, where are we going? This isn't the way home."

"No," he agreed. "It isn't, but we've both just had a big shock, and you need food."

"I had lunch before we left."

"Pregnant women need extra calories. Think of it as a reward for your overachieving uterus."

She snorted out a half laugh, half groan. "It's like my body heard about my fertility issues and my uterus said, 'hold my beer.' Silly womb." Her right hand rubbed over her stomach. "You didn't have to prove yourself this much."

Yes, there was that sass! He'd been worried in the doctor's office when she'd been so docile and spaced out. Not Pru at all. He much preferred her like this, fierce and feisty.

She sighed. "I really should get back to work, Finn."

"I know, but do you have to go back before enjoying some delicious chili cheese fries?"

From the corner of his eye, he saw her straighten.

"Chili cheese fries?"

"But if you're not hungry, I can just take you back home—"

"Keep driving, Jamison."

He chuckled, never once veering from his path. When he pulled into an empty space at the retro carhop drive-in, he ordered two lemonades, two cheeseburgers for himself, and an extra-large chili cheese fry for Pru.

"Extra-large?" she asked with a raised brow.

"You're eating for three."

At the reminder, her smile slipped.

"Twins," she said softly. "I can't believe it. How am I going to handle twins?"

He didn't think the words were directed at him, but he answered anyway. "You can handle anything. You're Prudence goddamn Carlson."

"That's not my middle name."

"No, it's Mabel, but you get mad at me every time I use it."

"Because it's a stupid name!"

"Not as dumb as Shakespeare." In addition to a love of art, his mother also had a thing for old, dead wordsmiths. Thank God his father convinced her that the greatest playwright of all time might not be the best first name for a kid born in the twentieth century.

"Touché."

She glanced up at him, naked worry etched in her gaze. Worry he knew she would only let a handful of people ever see. He considered himself honored and humbled to be included in that minuscule number.

"Finn, what am I going to do? I didn't plan for two babies."

"Plans change, Pru. You know that better than anyone."

It wasn't like her parents planned to die in that car crash. Aunt Rose hadn't planned on suffering and eventually succumbing to complications from dementia. Life rarely worked out like people planned. It just existed, and everyone was along for the ride.

"If anyone can handle this, it's you."

"You think so?"

"I know so, and I'll be here to help you."

Her mouth turned down into an adorable little frown.

"I'm supposed to do this myself." The words left her on a soft whisper.

"But you don't *have* to." He reached for her hand, relieved when she allowed him to grasp it and pull it to his chest. A spark of awareness shot through him at the touch. He saw her pupils dilate, fingers tightening in his as if she felt this strange energy, too. Was it simply leftover sexual tension from their night together or something more? Whatever it was, he couldn't deal with it at the moment. One crisis at a time.

"You're my best friend, Pru. We've been through a lot together, and I will always be here for you, no matter what you need. Even if these babies weren't mine, I'd still want to help in any way I could."

A furrow appeared on her brow, but he kept going.

"I know you want to do this alone, and I'm not stopping you. This is your journey. Your dream. But my mom always said she never could have handled raising us kids if it wasn't for all the support she got from her family and friends. I'm your friend, Pru."

Hell, they were practically family, for as long as they'd known each other.

"I won't take custody from you. I'd never do that. But those kids are a part of me, and I want to be in their life. I want to help as much as you'll let me."

He reached out with his free hand slowly, hovering over her abdomen. He watched her swallow, her eyes misting. He didn't move closer, waiting for her to take the lead. Finally, she reached out and grasped his hand, pulling it toward her and settling it low on her stomach.

"I...I think I really need your support and maybe a little bit of help, too."

He knew how hard it was for her to say those words.

"We're a team, Pru. This is your show, but I'm your backup. Like always. I'm here. We've already proved sex can't ruin friendship. Wanna prove two best friends can co-parent the crap outta kids?"

She laughed, a small tear sliding down her cheek. He released the hold he had on her hand and brushed it away with his thumb.

"You and me."

"This idea is either crazy or brilliant."

He grinned. "Let's go with brilliant, since I thought of it."

She rolled her eyes. "Crazy it is, then."

He laughed, grateful when she joined in.

Their food arrived, and he happily watched as Pru dug in to her chili cheese fries with gusto.

"Oh my God, this is amazing!"

She moaned, the sound reminding him of the sexy noises she made the night they were together. The night that led them here. He had to shift in his seat to hide the erection tenting his jeans. He promised to help her, not jump her.

He might still be aching to go there, but he wasn't going to put any pressure on Pru. She had enough to deal with right now. She didn't need the knowledge that one night with her wasn't enough to satisfy him.

Hell, he wasn't sure a hundred nights would do.

And what in the holy hell was he supposed to do with that information? Especially now? Maybe it was just Pru's pregnancy hormones rubbing off on him. That could happen, right? Sympathy pregnancy. He'd read about it in one of the books he'd gotten from the library, men taking on the physical symptoms of their partners.

Physical, jackass. Not emotional.

Okay, so he might, maybe, possibly, have a tiny thing for Pru.

Didn't matter. What mattered was what she wanted, and right now she wanted to eat chili cheese fries. So that's what Finn delivered. Beyond that, it was her call. Call him a chicken—and his jerk brothers often did—but he had never been one to rock the boat. His life was fine the way it was.

So what if he had secretly repressed feelings for his best friend who was carrying his twin babies but didn't want a relationship with him? As long as she was happy, he was happy.

Right?

Chapter Twelve

"Twins?"

"Yes," Pru sighed, answering Lilly for the third time that afternoon. After she'd eaten her weight in chili cheese fries, Finn had dropped her off at her place. There'd been a weird moment in the car where she would have sworn he was going to kiss her. Again. What made it even stranger was how much she wished he had.

It's just the baby hormones.

"Twins?"

"She's established it's twins." Mo laughed as she filled their office electric kettle with water. In deference to Pru's condition, they'd all switched from afternoon coffee to tea. "I think you broke Lilly with your news, Pru."

"I'm not broken." The dark-haired woman glared from behind her glasses. "I'm simply surprised."

"Not as surprised as me." Pru swore her brain shut down for a solid ten minutes after the doctor told her the news.

"How'd Finn take it?"

"He recovered from the shock quicker than I did."

Which freaked her out even more. She was supposed to be the one in control. The cool, calm, collected one. She'd planned for this. Not the whole *getting knocked up with twins by her best friend* thing, but the motherhood journey. To be honest, it kind of got under her skin that Finn seemed to be the one keeping his head while she constantly felt the rug being pulled out from under her. This wasn't the way things were supposed to go.

"I can see that." Mo grabbed the kettle when it clicked then poured the steaming hot water into three mugs. "He deals with high stress situations all the time. Finn's pretty good at keeping his cool."

Sure, but all the stress he dealt with mainly affected other people. He might be in the thick of it with a fire or emergency call, but then he got to go home to his life, where everything was the same.

She supposed this wasn't all too different. They'd agreed that even if Finn had fathered the baby—*babies*—this was her show. She wanted to be a mom, and while she agreed to let him help a little, it wasn't like they were moving in together or anything. So in a way, the whole twin thing wouldn't affect his daily life the way it would hers.

The thought made her feel slightly better. Finn wasn't freaking out because this was still her show, her plan. He wasn't trying to insert himself and take over. He wanted to help her, but he wasn't pushing her out of the way and assuming charge. It wouldn't change his life, so he had no reason to panic like she did.

The office phone rang, and Lilly answered.

"Mile High Happiness, this is Lilly speaking. How can we make your dreams come true?"

Dreams come true. Her dreams were coming true. Maybe not in the way she planned and maybe with an extra bonus dream, but they were happening. Funny how most people's dreams revolved around giving and accepting love, whether from a spouse, a child, a pet, or even just good friends. Pru might not believe in the happily-ever-afters they sold with their business—at least, not for her—but she did believe everyone deserved love in some form, however they wanted to accept it. And she wanted it from two soft, snuggly, sweet babies.

Her hand moved to her stomach, rubbing in circles. She couldn't believe there were two precious miracles in there.

"Peppermint tea," Mo whispered as she slid a mug of steaming, pungent liquid in front of Pru.

"Thanks."

They sipped their tea quietly, listening to Lilly talking with what sounded like a new client on the phone.

"Oh yes, the Rockies have spectacular views in August. Perfect time of year for an outdoor wedding."

"If you want to sweat your makeup off."

Mo chuckled at Pru's muttered statement. Lilly, however, did not find it as amusing.

"I would suggest a venue up in the mountains, as it would provide picturesque views, amazing photo opportunities, ample accommodations for out-of-town guests, and the weather will be slightly cooler at higher elevations."

This was why Lilly handled the clients and Pru handled the money. She was too logical to spin things. If a bride came up to her and said she wanted an outdoor wedding in Colorado during August—one of the hottest months of the year—she would tell the woman straight up how dumb an idea that was. Lilly had this magic touch. She could point out a problem without making it seem insurmountable.

Maybe Pru could learn a thing or two from her roommate. Perhaps Lilly could teach her how to remain cool in a crisis and not freak out every time her plan went awry. Because lately, that's all it seemed to be doing.

• • •

Two weeks after their appointment, Finn found himself pulling up in front of Pru's apartment building. They both had the day off and had decided to go to a few baby stores to start checking things out.

She might not want any help, but he'd be damned if he washed his hands of the whole matter and left her all on her own. He wasn't trying to horn in on her motherhood. He just wanted to help his friend. He'd be doing this even if those weren't his kids growing in her belly.

My kids.

It still freaked him out that he was going to be a father. He'd never imagined himself as a dad. Would they call him Dad? He had no idea. He didn't want to take anything away from Pru, but he did want…something. What, he wasn't exactly sure yet.

But something.

He couldn't deny the small ache in his chest whenever he thought about those two little babies. Would they have his eyes? His crooked smile? Would they come out as bald as the baby pictures he'd seen of Pru or with a solid head of blond fuzz like he'd had?

And would they love him?

Growing up, his dad had been his biggest hero. Still was. But his parents were in a loving, committed relationship and had been for decades. He loved Pru the way you do with good friends, but they weren't *in love*. They weren't going to be a happy family all living together having Sunday barbeques and Wednesday game nights. They also weren't going to be sharing custody, at odds and using the kids as leverage the way some broken relationships did.

Because they weren't a broken relationship. Or a happy marriage. They were something different, something better—

best friends. They could handle this, and that's why he wanted to be a part of everything. He just had to remember that whenever those odd pangs rose in his chest.

Pulling his cell from his pocket, he shot Pru a text.

F: *Downstairs. Want me to come up?*

P: *No, I'll be right down.*

True to her text, Pru came walking out the front door of the complex less than a minute later. She had on her college sweatshirt over a pair of black leggings and brown ankle boots, the pair his mother had given her for her birthday last year.

"Isn't it a little warm for a sweatshirt?" he asked as she hopped into the car.

Fall had arrived with the changing of months, but November still held temperatures in the high fifties to low sixties most days in Colorado. Not sweater weather by any means. Hell, he was still wandering around in shorts and T-shirt most days. He'd worn jeans today because he'd once again forgotten to do laundry and he was down to his last few clean items of clothing.

"The building is freezing," she complained, pulling the sweatshirt over and off her head. "The AC is cranked full blast because maintenance is doing a blow-out thing with the vents or something. I don't know. All I know is it's an iceberg in there."

He tried to respond, but his throat suddenly swelled to the point of closure. The moment Pru took her sweatshirt off, his eyes were drawn to her chest like a moth to a flame. Hard not to stare considering his best friend was spilling out of her low-cut V-neck T-shirt. The polite thing to do would be to look away, but he couldn't.

He remembered those breasts. He'd held them, tasted

them, reveled in their absolute magnificence. And there they were again, tempting him, causing a scorching fire low in his belly, making him burn and ache for just one more touch, one more taste.

"Finn, hello. Earth to Finn. Please pay attention to the woman attached to the boobs."

Heat rose on his face all the way to the tips of his ears. He shook his head, clearing his throat and somehow dragging his gaze from her chest to her face. Thankfully, Pru looked amused rather than pissed.

"Um, sorry." He shrugged, then decided he'd already been caught so he might as well ask. "Damn, Pru. Have they always been that big?"

She glanced down at her chest with a frown. "No. It's like they have a mind of their own. I'm growing out of all my bras, and these damn things keep popping out of my shirts like a wildly inappropriate game of peek-a-boob."

He couldn't stop a laugh from escaping his lips.

"It's not funny, Finn. Do you know how expensive bras are?"

No, they'd never been on his shopping list. He'd never even bought lingerie for a woman before, which had always seemed like a dick move to him. *Here, have some super uncomfortable underwear that I'm going to stare at for five seconds before I strip it off your body.* Why not just get naked? Naked was good.

And thinking of naked, underwear, and breasts while sitting a foot away from Pru, who was currently pregnant with his twins after they'd had a night of the most amazing sex he could remember in a damn long time, proved to be a very bad idea if the hardening of a certain part of his anatomy was anything to go by. He adjusted his position in the driver's seat, tamping down his inappropriate thoughts.

"So, where to?" he asked.

"Let's go to Colorado Mills. A new baby store just opened in the mall, and they're having a sale."

Sounded good to him.

They headed out of the city to the nearby suburb where the giant mall was located. Finn parked the car and followed Pru's lead as she navigated the massive building, heading with a focused purpose toward their destination.

"Hello, welcome to Then Comes Baby." A middle-aged woman with a pleasant smile and box braids pulled up into a high bun on the top of her head greeted them. "Can I help you find anything?"

"I saw online you were having a BOGO sale on baby clothes?"

The woman's smile grew as she glanced down to Pru's stomach. "Yes, dear. And all the sale items come with a thirty-day return policy with gift receipt. Shopping for someone else or yourself?"

"Me."

"Congratulations."

"It's twins." He had no idea why he blurted that out. Pru and the saleswoman had been handling the conversation fine, ignoring him completely. Maybe he just wanted to feel like a part of it all.

"Well, then." The woman's dark brows went up. "Mommy and Daddy certainly came to the right store. You're going to need two of everything."

Mommy and Daddy. That sounded… He wasn't quite sure. Not wrong, per se, but odd.

"Yup, two of everything."

He glanced over to Pru as those soft words left her with none of the usual bravado she normally spoke with. Her skin had paled. He didn't know if it was due to the Mommy and Daddy comment or the double baby reminder. He reached out, grasping her hand and bringing it to his lips. Her gaze shot to him in a question.

"Come on, *Mommy*. Let's go check out what we need for our little Thing One and Thing Two."

"Right this way," the helpful woman motioned for them to follow her to the back of the shop.

Finn started moving, tugging Pru along, since he still had her hand firmly clasped in his. She narrowed her gaze, mouthing something suspiciously close to *you're a dick* before coming along. Once the saleswoman had them settled in the clothing section, questions answered, she excused herself to help another customer who'd just come in. The second she left, a sharp sting hit his shoulder.

"Hey!" He glared at Pru, who yanked her hand from his. "Did you just smack me?"

"You deserve it, you ass."

"What did I do?"

"You made that sweet woman think we were some happy married couple with twins on the way."

Her color was back now, paleness replaced by the pink flush of frustration. A Finn specialty.

"I never said we were married, and we *are* having twins."

"No, *I'm* having twins. Even if we were a couple, I'm the one pushing these babies out of my vagina. Why does every man on earth insist on saying *we* in regard to pregnancy and having babies? I know there's an 'us' in uterus, but guys are there for the first five seconds of conception. I'm the one who's going to have to put ice packs on my crotch for a week after the birth."

He placed his hands on her hips, pulling her into him until her chest brushed against his. He willed his erection to settle down as the soft swell of her breast grazed him. Now was not the time.

"Five seconds, huh? To my recollection it lasted a lot longer than five seconds, and you sure seemed to enjoy the work I put into it."

"Finn? What are you doing?" The shaky question left her lips. Lips he was dying to taste again. Her pupils dilated as her gaze focused on his mouth, eyes heating with need. He felt the sharp points of her nipples as they hardened against him.

Shit.

This had started as a diversion tactic. A way to pull Pru back from the brink of the panic he'd seen in her eyes. He just wanted to help. Now he was horny as hell and propositioning his best friend in the middle of a baby store. Maybe he was the one who needed help.

Laughing softly, he took a small step back. "Just messing with you. Trying to lighten the mood so you don't go into panic mode."

The lust faded, replaced with irritation. "I wasn't going into panic mode."

He simply raised a brow.

"Okay, fine. I might have been panicking. A little. Slightly." She let out a deep sigh. "I really need to sit down and rework my plan now that it involves two babies. I might..." She bit her lip. "I may even need to move. With twice the stuff, I'll need much more room."

"Hey." He grabbed her hand again, this time tugging her in for a friendly hug. "You'll figure it out. You planned for this, remember? Nothing's changed too much, you just have to expand your original plan."

He felt the warm caress of her breath on his chest through his shirt as she sighed softly.

"You're right. Thanks, Finn. I know I tend to freak when my plans get altered."

She did, but that was just who she was, and he liked her that way. Wouldn't be Pru if she didn't flip a little bit.

They moved through the racks of clothing, picking a

few items to purchase and noting others to add to her baby registry. They also looked at the other baby items in the store, the strollers, car seats, change pads, carriers, bathing tubs. He had no idea babies needed so much stuff. After about an hour, his head started to spin.

"What the hell is this?"

Pru glanced at him with a smile as he grabbed two baby bottles attached to some kind of funnel things with tubes leading to a small box that looked like you could order HBO off it.

She laughed softly at his confused expression. "It's a breast pump."

Oh. That made sense, he supposed. Curious, he placed the funnel bottles on his chest. Huh, didn't seem too—

"What the hell?"

He tried to yank the device off as it suddenly started up, sucking his shirt and a good bit of flesh into the cups of the funnels.

"Pru!" He glared at her, and she doubled over with laughter. "It's not funny. Ow! This really—ow! Stings! Turn it off."

Still laughing, she slapped the button on the base, cutting off the powerful suction and releasing him from the pump's vacuum pull.

"I'm sorry, Finn." Pru laughed, turning down a dial that had been suspiciously set to maximum. "But you looked like you were going into full panic mode. It was a distraction."

Okay, he probably deserved that.

"Touché." He grinned. "You ready to go?"

"Yeah."

They paid for the items she'd picked out. She did, anyway, because she refused to let Finn help, claiming he drove here. Whatever—a few miles of gas did not equal the hundred dollars she spent on baby stuff. But he had to remind himself, this was her show and he promised to stand back and help with anything she wanted help with. Nothing more.

It was getting harder to remember he was simply a side player in all this when he found himself wanting to be more.

They headed back to the car, where he pulled out three more bags of the nausea pops from his trunk, which he'd bought earlier that week. She might not let him purchase any of the things for the baby, but she couldn't stop him from taking care of her. She thanked him with only a slight roll of her eyes, tucking the candy into her shopping bags.

"Thanks for coming with me today, Finn." She turned in her seat to face him when he parked in front of her building. "And thanks for helping me through my tiny, almost, not-really freak-out in the store."

He chuckled, knowing how much Pru hated to admit to any kind of weakness or need for help.

"You're welcome. I'd thank you for almost ripping my nipples off, but to be honest, it still kind of hurts. I'm going to have boob hickies for a week."

She laughed. "Oh, poor Finn. Want me to kiss them and make it better?"

She was teasing, but the thought of Pru's lips on his bare skin again shot a bolt of desire straight to his groin. It must have shown on his face, because her laughter died. Her tongue came out to drag along her lower lip in an unconscious, sexy move that made him hard as hell.

Screw it. He needed one more taste.

He cupped the back of her neck with his palm, pulling her forward. Her hands landed on his chest, lightly rubbing over skin that was sensitive in no way due to his experience with the breast pump and in every way because of the sexy, tempting, confusing woman before him. He stared into her dark brown eyes, asking the question without using words.

"Kiss me, Finn."

She knew what he wanted without him even having to say it, because she wanted it, too. They were both screwed up. So why not be confused together?

He dipped his head, capturing her lips with his, reveling in the soft, mewling moan of hers that filled his ears as he took the kiss deeper. She opened for him, hands sliding up his chest and neck to rub against the buzzed sides of his hair. Yes! This was what he needed. The sweet, heavenly taste of Pru was a balm to all the confusing swirling mess of emotions that had been rioting inside him for weeks.

A horn blared behind them, breaking the spell. Pru pulled away, fingers leaving his scalp to rub over her swollen lips. Lips red and plump from his kisses. A blur of motion caught the corner of his eye as someone rushed by them to hop in the very rude and loudly honking taxi behind them.

"Okay, so, that was…" Pru shook her head and quickly gathered her bags then opened the car door and hopped out. "Bye, Finn."

Bye, Finn? She kissed the holy hell out of him, and now she was running away like his car was on fire. If it was, the firefighter in him knew how to put it out. But damn if the aching, confused man inside knew how to extinguish this burning need he'd suddenly developed for his best friend.

He watched as she hurried into the building, stepping into the empty elevator and staring back at him with hungry, questioning eyes.

"Bye, Pru," he whispered to the empty car, watching as the elevator doors closed, wishing he knew the answers to the questions those dark eyes asked.

Chapter Thirteen

The past few weeks, Pru had been waking in the middle of the night with nausea or the urgent need to pee. Tonight, something entirely different and much more irritating was keeping her from slipping into slumber land. Grabbing her phone from the bedside table, she groaned when the screen lit up to show a time just after midnight. Her groan turned into a growl as she focused on her lock screen picture—an adorable shot of her favorite, furry, four-legged creature in the arms of the very reason Pru couldn't sleep.

Finn.

Why the hell had she kissed him earlier? Why had he kissed her back? And why for the love of all the chili cheese fries in the world had it been so damn hot that she lay there, hours later, going over the damn thing in her mind? Replaying the kiss made her remember other kisses in other places on other nights.

"Yeah, and look where that got me."

Her hand unconsciously rubbed her stomach. She'd noticed a slight bulging to her abdomen in the past few days, evident by the fact she couldn't fit into any of her jeans lately. Good thing she had a drawer full of leggings. Her doctor told Pru she might start to show earlier with twins, and the doc had been right. Everything seemed to be happening faster, more intensely than she planned. She hadn't even suspected she'd be pregnant yet but figured it would take at least two tries before she conceived.

But I didn't even get to the "try" part, did I?

No, she had not. Which brought her right back around to her dilemma: the kiss in the car with Finn. Obviously, they hadn't scratched their itch as well as they thought. Or she hadn't. As much as it pained her to admit it, Pru still craved Finn's touch. More so now, since she knew how electrifying it could be.

Shit.

What was she going to do? She had a box full of fun under her bed, a few faithful toys she'd collected over the years when good men were scarce and desires needed tending. The only problem? She'd already tried it. Before she slipped into bed, she'd retrieved the box full of fun and taken care of business. Usually after a self-care session, she'd be good for a few days. So why was she tossing and turning and wishing she had Finn conveniently stashed under her bed instead of the Butterfly Fly Flirt 3000?

"I need some tea."

Like tea would help anything. What she really needed was a shot of vodka, but since that wasn't happening for at least another year or so, she'd have to settle for some soothing chamomile. Tossing off her covers, she threw on her robe and headed for the kitchen. She filled the electric kettle and grabbed a mug and the tea box, all the while cursing Finn and his stupid, sexy…sexiness under her breath.

The kettle clicked over. Pru placed a tea bag in her mug, pouring the steaming hot water over it and gagging at the smell. She knew chamomile was supposed to calm frazzled nerves, but the stuff smelled like garden mulch. Didn't taste much better. But since all the pregnancy books told her she needed to stay as calm as possible over the next few months to ensure a healthy growing environment for her babies, she could suck down some calming weed water. For her babies.

Didn't mean she couldn't try to make the best of it.

She wrenched open the cabinet by the fridge, pushing aside various bottles of herbs and cooking oils they rarely used in her search for sweetness. "Where's the damn honey?"

"In the pantry by the peanut butter."

Pru held back a small scream; it stuck in her throat, making her sound like Bruiser whenever a bigger dog pounced on her at the park.

"Lilly!" She brought a hand to her racing heart, glaring at her roommate. "You scared me half to death."

One dark brown eyebrow rose. "Me? I'm not the one ransacking our kitchen at midnight, waking everyone up thinking there's a burglar in the apartment."

"And what exactly would a criminal want to steal from us?" Mo sauntered into the kitchen, arms stretching as her jaw opened wide with a yawn. "Our ten-year-old TV? My crappy laptop that has a battery so old it can't keep a charge and needs to be plugged in to work? Our shoes? Wait, scratch that last one. I would totally steal your shoe collection, Lilly."

The tall, slim woman pointed a finger in Mo's direction. "You keep your clodhoppers away from my shoes. You'll stretch them out, Bigfoot."

"Ouch! Where's the love, Lil?"

"It's twelve eighteen in the morning. I save all my love-giving for after the sunrise."

Only Lilly would know the exact time even in the middle of the night. Morning. Whatever.

"I'm sorry, guys." Pru closed the cabinet, shoulders

sinking in defeat. "I didn't mean to wake you. You can go back to bed. Everything is fine."

Her friends shared a look. Next thing she knew, Mo was gently leading her to the table while Lilly grabbed the honey from the pantry, filling two more mugs with hot water and tea bags and bringing everything over. They sat around the table like it was the middle of the day instead of pitch-black night.

"So what's up? Besides us, I mean." Mo grinned.

"It's nothing." She was just being dumb, hormonal, whatever. She had no idea. "I just…I kissed Finn."

"Yeah, we know. That's kind of how all this happened." Mo gestured to Pru's stomach.

"No. I mean I kissed Finn today. When he dropped me off after shopping and…"

Mo waved a hand in the air. "And?"

"And some flirting? I think. I don't know. It's all weird."

"Of course it is, sweetie." Lilly pushed her glasses up her nose. "You slept with your best friend, and now you're having his baby. Babies. That would be an odd situation for anyone."

"So is all this new chemistry because of the baby hormones or what?" Pru asked.

"I highly doubt that, considering you slept with him before you had the baby hormones to blame." Mo shoved her riot of multicolored curls over one shoulder.

"I'm not blaming the hormones for *that*, Moira."

One pale blond eyebrow rose. "Really? Cause it sure sounds like you are. And that's fine if that's how you want to play it, but don't get mad at Finn for being all hot and sexy and keeping you up at night with longing."

"I am not up longing for Finn's sexiness."

Her roommates simply stared at her. She raised her mug to her lips, but the steam rising from the cup warned her it was still too hot to drink. Setting it back down, she gave in to the silent treatment.

"Okay, fine! Maybe I found Finn attractive before he knocked me up, and maybe the sex was amazing, and maybe I want to do it again, but that doesn't mean I should."

Mo shrugged. "Why not?"

Flabbergasted, she turned to Lilly. "Could you help me out here?"

"Sorry, sweetie, but I actually agree with her."

"Twice in the same year. That's gotta be a record."

Lilly sighed, ignoring Mo's gleeful comment. "I'll be the first person in the world to tell you that sexual liaisons can have very dire consequences."

Lilly would know. The incident a few years ago that almost ruined their budding business still hung like a weight around the woman's neck no matter how many times Pru and Moira assured her she'd done nothing wrong.

"Lilly, it wasn't your—"

"No." A firm hand rose to cut Pru off. "This isn't about me and my past mistakes. This is about you and your current situation. The cat is already out of the bag, Prudence. You and Finn engaged in intercourse, and that resulted in a lifelong tie between you. Now, I know you two don't plan on cohabitating or starting a romantic relationship, but you already have a connection. A friendship. And if the first time didn't cause irreparable damage, then it stands to reason a subsequent time wouldn't, either."

Trust Lilly to logic sex out.

"I say bone him again."

And trust Mo to bring it all back to basics.

"It's your decision," Lilly continued, giving Pru's hand a gentle squeeze. "Well, yours and Finn's. But as long as you both agree to what you're doing, I don't see why you have to deny yourselves what you want."

They'd agreed the first time on what they wanted. Could they really pursue a sex-only relationship while keeping their friendship intact on top of her having his twins?

"I'm getting a headache thinking through all this," she groaned.

"So don't think." Mo patted her hand. "Just go with what you feel."

What she felt? She felt horny as ever, and the only thing, the only person, who could possibly satisfy her was probably snoring away in his bed less than a mile away. Jerk. Why should he get to sleep soundly while she was up? Technically, he caused her situation, at least partially, so he should take care of it.

The logic didn't quite make sense, but she didn't care.

"How late is too late for a booty call?"

Mo snickered. "Please, if it's before one a.m., it doesn't even count as a booty call. You're still on 'Netflix and Chill' time."

A smile curled her lips. "Then it's a good thing Finn has streaming."

Her roommates grinned, toasting her with their tea as she rose from the table and headed to her room to change. In less than ten minutes she'd put on a pair of black leggings and a large sweater—forgoing a bra since she was just going to take it off anyway—and driven over to Finn's. Luckily, his building had guest parking, and there was one slot left. She parked, quickly making her way to his apartment and, thinking she'd need to rouse him from a peaceful sleep—*ass*—she pounded on the door.

The door swung open before her third knock. Finn stood there in a pair of jeans that rode so low on his waist, they were in danger of falling off. His chest was bare. Her mouth salivated, resolve in her decision firming up at the glorious sight before her.

"Pru? What's wrong?"

"I'm horny, and it's your fault!"

Shock and confusion replaced concern on his stupid handsome face. She barreled into his apartment, careful not to touch his naked flesh. The moment she did, all bets would be off, and she'd rather not jump him in the hallway where anyone passing could see.

"Say that again?"

The sound of the door closing and locking hit her ears. She glanced around, noticing Bruiser sleeping soundly in her fluffy doggy bed at the foot of Finn's. The room was dark save for the dim glow coming from the television playing some nature documentary. So, it seemed she wasn't the only one awake tonight. Good. No need for her to suffer this craving alone. No need for either of them to suffer, according to her friends.

Her very smart friends.

She turned to face Finn and repeated her earlier statement. "I'm horny, and it's your fault."

His eyebrows pinched together. "Okay. What do you want me to do about it?"

"Me."

"Huh?"

Ugh! Men could be so dense.

"Me. I want you to do me. I want to have sex. Again. With you." Best to clarify since his cognitive skills seemed to be running a little behind tonight.

Now his dark blond brows rose, climbing up his forehead as her demand sank in.

"You want to have sex? With me?"

"No, with Trevor Noah. I thought you could introduce us."

He grinned at the mention of her Hollywood crush, who he in no way knew or could introduce her to.

"Smartass."

"Seriously, Finn." She sighed, dropping all pique. "I don't

know if it's the baby hormones, or if once wasn't enough, or… The itch is still there. I just want you again. Do you still want me?"

He crossed the small space between them in less than two long strides. She had to tilt her head back to gaze up into his handsome face. His bright gaze burned with the same hunger, the same fire she'd seen the first time they were together.

First and hopefully not last.

Because she really, really wanted more. But the question was, did he?

"I want you, Pru." He cupped her cheek in his hand.

Hallelujah!

"I haven't been able to stop thinking about that night since it happened. We were good together." His other hand came up to rest low on her belly. "Maybe a little too good."

She laughed, placing her hands over his on her stomach. Something warm and sharp, having nothing to do with the sexual need burning deep inside, filled her chest. She pushed the strange emotion away. This wasn't about feelings. Well, it was, but not those kind. This was about physical pleasure. Nothing more.

"I don't want to confuse anything." He spoke the words softly. At her raised brow, he chuckled. "Any more than it already is."

"But you want me." A statement, not a question, since he'd just said so a moment ago.

His smile dimmed, his mouth firming the way it did when he denied himself something he wanted. Her. It dawned that what he wanted was her, and he'd been denying himself. Why?

The reasons were obvious. They were friends, she was pregnant—with his kids—and she knew he didn't want to pile more onto her already full plate. Finn never pushed his wants on others. He was always the one who took care of everyone else, regardless of what he desired.

That was changing. Right now.

Stepping back, she tugged her sweatshirt over her head, letting it drop to the floor. She stood there in nothing but her leggings, delighting in the ravenous heat burning in Finn's eyes as he stared at her unfettered breasts.

"You're topless."

"Thanks for the update." She glanced pointedly at his naked chest. "Thought I'd join the club."

He grinned at her joke. "You're making it awfully hard to be a gentleman, Pru."

"I didn't come here for a gentleman. I came here for sex."

His hands reached out, grasping her hips and tugging her to him until their naked skin pressed together. She let out a needy moan as the sensitive tips of her nipples collided with his hard, warm chest. His head bent down, lips caressing hers in a barely-there kiss.

"Do you want to talk about this first?"

She reached up, wrapping her arms around his neck as she spoke against his mouth, "Sex first. Talk later."

And being the amazing best friend he was, Finn catered to her demand by using those lips for something other than words as, finally, he gave her the deep and thorough kiss she'd been craving.

Yes! Her box full of fun had nothing on Finn.

Chapter Fourteen

Pru was right. Talk was overrated. Actions were better.

Much, much better, he mused as his hands slipped from her hips to curve around her backside and cup the firm, round globes of her ass. A slight squeak escaped her lips, and he swallowed the sound, thrusting his tongue against hers, reveling in her eagerness as she lifted her legs, attempting to climb his body like a flagpole.

A sharp, high-pitched bark caused him to leave the heaven of Pru's mouth. Finn turned his head to stare down at Bruiser. They must have woken the poor pup, who tilted her head, looking slightly confused.

"It's okay, Bru Baby. Go back to sleep."

Bruiser made a soft whine, head tilting in the opposite direction.

"I'm fine, Bruiser. Your daddy is just…helping me with a problem."

"Horniness is a problem?"

"It is when it keeps me up at night."

He couldn't stop the smug satisfaction from turning his

lips up. "Aw, thinking about my sexy bod kept you up?"

With a mulish expression, she said nothing, simply pointed to his TV still playing the ocean documentary he had in no way been watching but had turned on because he'd needed a distraction himself. He shrugged, the move made slightly more difficult by the fact that he had his sexy, pregnant best friend in his arms.

"Okay, you got me. I thought the dulcet voice of Attenborough would soothe my unsatisfied body to sleep."

She grinned. "Let's take this over to the bed, and I'll make sure we're both so satisfied we sleep for days."

He raised a brow. "Quite the boast."

She leaned forward, gently nipping his earlobe before soothing the tiny sting with a soft kiss. Raw heat shot straight down his spine to the hardening spot between his legs, where he swore he could feel that tempting kiss.

"Not a boast if it's true." Her lips nuzzled his neck, kissing, sucking, taking small love bites as she drove him out of his freaking mind. "Go to sleep, Bruiser."

His dog, too tired from her earlier trip to the park—way to go, Past-Finn, for that excursion—followed Pru's orders, turning around in her little doggy bed three times before lying down. Her soft puppy snores melted in with the sounds of the city at night filtering through his apartment windows. He walked Pru the few steps it took to get to his bed. Never before had he been so grateful for his tiny living accommodations. As primed as he was, he didn't think he could make it across a huge apartment to a bedroom. How convenient to be only feet away from heaven.

Scratch that.

Heaven was in his arms.

They reached the bed, Pru's tongue working magic on him, making it near impossible for him to move, but he did. He had to, or he was going to lose control. Gently, he leaned down and placed her on the bed, grabbing her leggings and stripping them off, leaving her gloriously naked. Her shoes had fallen off…somewhere in the short trip across his studio. He didn't know or care where at the moment. The only thing filling his vision was the goddess lying below him.

"Your turn," she said.

She reached up to grasp the button of his jeans, but he placed a hand over hers. "Wait."

"Why?"

Because if she got her hands on him, they'd both be very disappointed in the next two minutes. He hadn't been with anyone since Pru. At first he thought it was just the weirdness he had to get over from sleeping with his best friend, then he assumed it was the emotions he was dealing with, realizing he was going to be a father, but truthfully, if he really looked deep down inside, there was another reason he hadn't taken anyone else to his bed.

Since that night with Pru, he'd found himself burning with need, but for only one woman. The one lying beneath him. He craved her, but he'd be damned if he didn't make her go out of her mind with pleasure before he sated his own desires.

"I need to taste you first. Please, Pru."

Her gaze turned hazy, filling with need. That small pink tongue darted out, rasping along her bottom lip. "Where?"

"Everywhere."

She shifted on the bed, stretching out, arms above her head, legs parting slightly, back arching to press those sweet, full breasts into the air like an offering. An offering he was desperate to accept.

"Since you asked so nicely."

The sly grin on her face was the first thing he craved, an appetizer as he worked his way down her body to the main course. He leaned over, capturing the clever mouth that could bring him to his knees with nothing but a touch or a word. She moaned deep in her throat, pressing up against him, wrapping one bare leg around his denim-clad one. *Damn!* The sexy minx was going to make him lose his focus. His focus being her. Her pleasure first. Everything else could come after.

Releasing her lips, he gently pried the silky-smooth leg from around him, placing it back on the soft mattress. His hands moved over her skin, trembling a bit at the heat emanating from her, the sparks, the connection. Yes! This… this was what he'd been aching for. The sharp bolt of rightness he felt when touching her. The strange duality of electricity and absolute comfort in pleasuring Prudence Carlson.

"Finn!"

She cried out his name as he moved down her body, sampling the sweet pulse point rapidly beating at the base of her neck before going lower to capture one perfect, stiff, dusty-rose–colored nipple between his lips. He bit down softly, wrenching another loud moan from her. Her hips moved against him in a silent plea.

He'd get there. In time. He didn't want to rush this. Sure, she'd come to him tonight, but what about tomorrow? If tonight was all he got of Pru, he was damn sure going to make it last.

"Like that?" He blew against her breast, glossy and wet from his kiss, moving to the other with a chuckle when she lightly smacked his shoulder.

"Don't fish for compliments. You know I— Oh!"

Her words died off as he lavished the same attention on her other nipple. He continued down her body, loving the salty, sweet taste of skin that smelled of nothing more than Pru because he knew she preferred fragrance-free soaps. She didn't need them. Pru had a scent all her own. A natural, wild scent that reminded him of the clean, crisp Colorado air after a rain. Pure Pru.

When he reached her stomach, he paused at the slight swell of her belly, the reality of the moment crashing down around him. But an odd thing happened. It didn't frighten him. Quite the opposite.

Hovering there, poised above Pru, staring down at her magnificent naked body and knowing that small bump held two precious lives—two lives he helped create—caused something deep within him to settle. To click into place. An overwhelming sense of rightness lodged within in his chest. His protective streak had always run a mile wide. Probably why he'd become a firefighter. But he knew, in that moment, he would do anything, *anything*, to ensure the health and happiness of these three souls.

His hand reached out to gently brush over her stomach, lips reverently kissing the tiny baby bump.

"Hey, you two. Mommy and Daddy are going to enjoy a little adult time right now, so you be good and, uh, go to sleep or whatever."

"Did you just tell our unborn babies to go to sleep so we can have sex?"

He smiled, not mentioning her use of the word *our.*

"I don't even think they've developed ears yet, Finn."

He shrugged. "I don't know what they're capable of deciphering from the womb. People say playing Mozart to the stomach makes them smarter and shit. Maybe they can hear sex noises, too."

"You really know how to set the mood. No wonder you never go past a first date."

He cut off her complaints with a soft stroke of his tongue between her legs. Her head dropped back, a low, keening cry escaping her lips.

"What was that again?"

"Nothing," she panted. "I said nothing. Continue on."

He chuckled, keeping his lips close enough for her to enjoy the vibrations. And she did enjoy them, if the hand currently grasping his hair and tugging him closer was any indication. Far be it from him to deny a lady's request.

He pressed closer, listening to her every sound as he added just the right amount of pressure with his mouth and hands to send her muscles tightening and her voice crying out moments later with her release. He stayed where he was, gentling her down from the explosive orgasm until she shifted beneath him.

"My turn."

"Your—" But that was all he got out before she twisted, pushing down on his shoulder until he toppled back on the bed with her rising above him, a move she could only execute because he allowed it. And why wouldn't he? He was all for letting this sexy, feisty woman have her way with him.

...

Pru stared down at Finn and the smug, crooked grin on his face. Okay, so the man had a reason to be smug. Holy hell, but that had been one amazing orgasm. Too bad it hadn't sated her need.

No, she wanted more. Guess she'd just have to continue their little game of touchy feely. Only now she got to do the touching and tasting. Her mouth salivated as she let her gaze wander over the sharp planes and honed muscles covered in a smattering of dark ink.

Who would have thought the bad-boy look would turn her on?

"You gonna stare all night or what?"

She answered by reaching back and cupping a very hard part of his anatomy, earning her a very creative four-letter curse, which she fully intended to fulfill before the night was over. But first she wanted to take a tour of naked Finn flesh. Fair was fair, after all.

She followed his pattern, paying less attention to his nipples and focusing instead on those scrumptious, rock-hard abs. There was a reason those annual firefighter charity calendars raised so much money, and those mouthwatering reasons were currently under her tongue.

Her hands moved down, unfastening the button of his jeans, lowering the zipper—slowly, because she enjoyed the tormented, needy expression in his eyes. He lifted his hips when she tugged, helping her pull the pants down his legs and tossing them off. No underwear for Finn. Lucky her.

She glanced down at the present she'd unwrapped. Lucky her, *indeed*. Taking him in her hand, she stroked, fascinated by the feel of something so soft and yet so hard.

"Pru," he groaned out a warning, but she'd never been very good at listening to others. She had her own mind. Her own plans. And her current plan was to drive Finn out of his mind the way he'd done to her.

"Oh, hell!" He swore as she took him in her mouth, gifting him with the same mind-blowing pleasure he'd bestowed on her.

"Precious, stop. I won't last."

That was okay. She was thoroughly enjoying herself, and they had all night.

"Pru, seriously. I need to be inside you."

Since she needed the exact same thing, she released him, rising to her knees and positioning herself above him. She paused, a thought flying thorough her mind that made her giggle.

"What?"

"Nothing, I was just thinking, um, guess we don't really need to worry about the condom anymore."

His grin widened as his hand came up to cover her belly

in a protective gesture. "Nope."

His thumb stroked, his eyes filling with serene happiness she'd never witnessed from her best friend before as he gazed at her small baby bump. Emotions clogged her throat, moisture gathering in her eyes, but she blinked back the tears. Baby hormones. That's all it was. This wasn't about emotions or feelings; it was just sex. Okay, some feelings, but the tingly-in-your-pants kind, not the flutter-in-your-heart kind.

She pressed down, taking him inside her inch by delicious inch. His hands flew out to grasp her hips as she fully settled, rocking against him.

"Pru."

Her name on his lips, uttered with such stark need, had her moving. Placing her hands on his chest, she set a slow rhythm that didn't last. With each thrust she became desperate, needy, hungry. They moved together, racing for that ultimate moment when pleasure would overwhelm to the point of pure ecstatic bliss.

She could sense the impending nirvana, just out of reach, the tiny buzz of fulfillment growing with each shift of their bodies until it exploded. Her entire body tensed as the wave crashed over her, her mouth falling open on a scream Finn silenced as he pulled her to him, capturing her lips, finding his own release.

They lay together, Pru sprawled on top of Finn as their frantic breathing evened out. His hands cradled her, holding her so protectively she wanted to cry.

No.

That was just the release of oxytocin from the amazing orgasm—orgasms—she'd just had.

"Stay?" Finn asked in the darkness. "Stay the night?"

Her bones were mush. She couldn't leave even if she wanted, and she found she didn't want.

"Okay, but I demand doughnuts in the morning."

He chuckled, his warm breath stirring the fine hairs at her brow. "Anything you want, Precious."

For right now, she wanted him.

"Finn?"

"Hmmm?"

"Can we… Do you want to…"

"Keep doing this?"

Thank God he seemed to be on the same wavelength.

"I've read that libido can increase in pregnant women. I don't want to go trolling for creepy dudes who get off on doing pregnant women, and my solo efforts don't seem to be as effective at getting the job done, so…"

Silence filled the dark room. The distant sounds of police sirens filtered in from the window, but the only light came from cars passing along the busy city roads underneath Finn's dark curtains.

Finally, his deep voice filled her ear. "You want to keep having sex because of the baby hormones?"

Did he sound a little…hurt? No, that was crazy. Finn didn't let emotions into his bed. Emotions led to permanence, and he'd made it very clear over the years how he felt about permanent relationships.

"Only if you want to. I mean, we certainly have chemistry."

"We're a five-alarm fire, Precious."

The dark words rumbled in her ear, sending a shiver of need down her spine even though she would have sworn she couldn't be aroused any more tonight.

"So, you're in? For more sex? With me, I mean?"

He laughed softly, the vibrations hitting her directly between her legs, though his lips caressed her neck.

"For you, Pru? I'd do damn near anything."

She chose to ignore the wealth of possibility in that statement and focused on the part she wanted. The more sex part. They were already having twins together. Finn wanted to be a part of the babies' lives. Why couldn't they add hot, wild sex to the equation, too?

"So that's a yes?"

"That's a hell yes. Under one condition."

Damn him. What guy put conditions on hot sex? Her best friend, apparently.

"What?"

She couldn't exactly see his face in the dark, but when he cupped her cheek, thumb stroking along her jaw, she knew he must have his serious face on. She could hear it in his tone as he made his request.

"No one else. It's only you and me, Pru. Until…until we go back to being just friends."

Could they ever go back to being *just friends* when they were having kids together? She hoped so, because the one thing in her life she couldn't lose was Finn. He'd been a part of her since she lost her parents, through the loss of Aunt Rose, through every heartbreak and struggle. She couldn't lose him because of a little sex, and she wouldn't. They could be friends and co-parents and sex buddies. And she would ignore that inner voice laughing its head off at her naivete right now.

"I already told you I'm not trolling for weird fetish dudes. The question is, can you give up the ladies?"

He lightly smacked her ass, swallowing her shriek as he pressed his lips against hers.

"There's only one lady I want at the moment, and she's right here, being a smartass."

Took one to know one. "Okay, then."

"Good. Then, we're agreed."

"Agreed. Now, should we get some rest?"

She felt his smile against her lips as his hand moved down to cup her right between her thighs.

"I find I'm still not sleepy. You?"

She sucked in a gasp as one long finger pressed inside. "N-no. Not sleepy."

"Good." The word rumbled in her ear. "Then let's see if I can make you scream again."

"I did not scream!"

But she had, and true to his word, Finn made her scream a few more times before they both slipped into exhausted, happy slumber.

Chapter Fifteen

"Hey, Pru, did you get the check from Missy Gunderson for the venue deposit?"

Pru glanced up from her laptop—which was totally displaying accounts receivable spreadsheets and *not* the Top 100 Unique Baby Names—to see Lilly shuffling through a stack of papers on her desk with a frown.

"Yes. I sent it off to the venue. The receipt is in the blue folder, but I already scanned it and put it in our electronic files."

Lilly had them back everything up—colored file folders for all payments, contracts, schedules, etc., then all that paper trail scanned and uploaded to multiple save spots including the cloud. Pru might be the planner, but Lilly was the paranoid one.

"Oh, right." Lilly frowned, exchanging the green folder she had open for the closed blue one in the small filing cabinet under the desk.

"I thought Pru was supposed to be the one with pregnancy brain." Mo chuckled. "You having sympathy symptoms, Lil?"

"Did you place the flower order for the Nguyen-Smith wedding?" Lilly asked, ignoring Mo's question.

"Yes. And it's a good thing the wedding is small." The blond woman frowned. "Mrs. Porter won't admit it, but her arthritis is really hurting her these days. The woman needs to hire on new help."

Agatha Porter was a sweet older woman they'd been in business with since they started Mile High Happiness. Pru loved the kind woman who reminded her very much of Aunt Rose, but she had noticed a drop in the woman's flower quality. Business was business, but it didn't sit right with her, or any of them, to stop sending customers to the woman simply because her health was failing her. Still, maybe Mo was right. Perhaps they should check in and try to convince Agatha it was time to hire on some help. She couldn't run the flower shop forever.

Her phone chimed, reminding her of her afternoon appointment.

"Oh, shoot. I gotta go." She stood, shutting down her laptop and grabbing her purse. "I'll be back later tonight."

"Have fun at baby class," Mo said with a cheery smile.

She waved at Mo, Lilly too deep in her folders to acknowledge her with more than a muttered goodbye.

Could one have fun at baby class?

Because she liked to be prepared in all situations, Pru had signed them up for a three-month course of weekly, hour-long classes that promised to cover everything from the birth process to baby safety and basic first aid. Not that Finn would need that section of the class, being a firefighter with EMT training, but she did, and skill refreshers never hurt.

Finn was just getting off his two-day shift, so Pru drove over to his place to pick him up. It had been two weeks since they decided that, in addition to friendship and him helping her with some baby stuff, they'd toss sex into the mix. And she had to admit, it was working out great. Better than great.

She spent most nights at his place—even when he stayed at the firehouse, she'd started staying at his apartment and taking care of Bruiser, who had developed a protective streak a mile wide. The tiny pup curled up on her lap anytime she sat down, resting her furry head right on Pru's belly. Silly dog thought the twins were her puppies.

Plus, Finn always brought home her favorite foods when his shifts were over. They'd sit on his couch watching TV and eating chili cheese fries—hey, the babies craved them; who was she to deny her unborn children what they wanted?— while Finn rubbed her feet, something that inevitably led to him rubbing other things. Every night would end with them in bed together. Even the nights they didn't have sex, Finn would pull her close, his hand resting protectively on her belly as his warmth lulled her to sleep.

Dating her best friend was awesome.

Whoa.

No, no, no. She wasn't *dating* Finn. They weren't in a relationship or anything. They were… She had no idea what they were, but they weren't dating. That was just weird.

Weirder than having sex with him almost every night and gestating his twins?

Okay, fine. Maybe they were dating.

Sort of.

But not really.

Should she…should she ask him about it? They hadn't really talked about what they were doing, save for agreeing that they'd only be doing it with each other. She certainly wasn't seeing anyone else, and she knew Finn wasn't either. So, did that mean they were seeing each other?

No. They were not dating. Full stop. The very thought was ridiculous. They wanted different things. Pru needed a partner who would be home every night. Someone who didn't risk death every time he went to work. She knew the pain caused by the loss of a parent. All her life she'd felt as though a piece of her soul was missing, dead and buried along with her mom and dad. She didn't want that for her own children.

She knew life could take anyone at any time, but why up the risks? The very reason Finn didn't want anything long term was the exact same reason she didn't want anything permanent with him, either.

Ugh! All this thinking was making her hungry. Or maybe that was the twins.

She parked at his place, heading up because, even though she'd gone just a half hour ago, Pru needed to pee, one of the downsides to this whole motherhood journey. She swore she was this close to buying one of those stadium bag things so she could pee wherever. She cringed when she thought about how much worse it would get.

"Worth it," she whispered, rubbing her belly.

She headed into Finn's building, using her key when she arrived at his door. It was only recently that Pru felt comfortable letting herself in on a daily basis. Sharing a bed opened up a whole new world of comfort between them she'd never known was missing.

As she stepped into the small studio, the sound of the shower running hit her ears, quickly followed by a happy, high-pitched bark and the furious clacking of nails on the hardwood floor

"There's my girl." She closed the door, bending down to scoop up Bruiser, who thankfully weighed less than five pounds. If the dog had been a husky or lab, she might have knocked Pru over with her enthusiastic greeting. "Do you need a treat?"

The Yorkie mix licked her chin before tucking her nose to sniff Pru's belly, nuzzling the growing bump, saying hi to the babies. She rose with the dog in the crook of her arm, heading to Finn's cupboard to get the sweet pup a treat. She was a pushover for a cute face.

Her kids were going to wrap her around their tiny, adorable fingers.

"Hey, Precious."

Strong, warm, slightly wet arms wrapped around her from behind. Finn's firm lips placed a soft kiss on the nape of her neck. Mmm, yummy. She hadn't even heard the shower shut off.

Bruiser gave out a small yip, tiny doggy legs whirling in the air, an indication she wanted no part of the human smooching and would rather be let down. Pru apologized to the pup and set her gently on the floor. Then turned in Finn's arms to plant a proper hello kiss to his delicious lips.

The kiss quickly deepened, heated. His hands came down to cup and squeeze her backside while she enjoyed a tactile tour of his damp, bare chest. As her hands traveled southward, she noticed he only had a towel wrapped around his hips.

Hello, easy access!

"How much time do we have before the class?"

"Enough for a quickie," she whispered against his smiling lips. "Give me thirty seconds. When I come out of the bathroom, I expect to find you naked on the bed."

"Yes, ma'am."

It was amazing what the man could do to her body in ten minutes. Pru never would have thought it possible, but they left fifteen minutes later, Finn fully dressed, her fully sated from not one but *two* orgasms.

The baby class was at the hospital ten minutes away. They arrived with one minute to spare.

Totally worth it.

"Hello, everyone, and welcome." The instructor, a small woman with gray hair and kind eyes, waved them all over.

"Take a seat around the circle and let's all introduce ourselves and give our due dates."

They went around the circle with introductions. There were a few married couples, a woman with her mother, whose husband was on deployment overseas, a pair of husbands with their surrogate, and Finn and her. It struck Pru that, while they were a kind of couple, they didn't have the same relationship everyone else in the room seemed to have.

Sure, they were sleeping together and had been friends forever, but there was something each of the other couples had that they didn't. And she didn't mean marriage. Having witnessed hundreds of weddings in the past few years, she knew a piece of paper was just that. She and the girls could tell within a week of working with a couple if they would last past the "I dos."

No, it wasn't the rings on their fingers that bothered her. So, what was it?

As the class continued, she shoved off the hinky feeling and concentrated on what the instructor was teaching them. They went through calming breathing exercises, pressure-point touch massage that claimed to reduce pain during labor, and different birthing positions. Throughout, the instructor asked questions to test the class's knowledge, and Pru found herself surprised by how much Finn knew. He seemed to raise his hand every time, nailing the answer.

"When did you become Dr. Baby?" she whispered.

He shrugged, continuing the lower back massage the instructor had taught them. "I've got some books at the firehouse that I've been reading in my down time."

He what now? Finn was reading baby books? In high school, he always rented the movies instead of reading their assignments for English. Made for a very strange book report when they'd studied *The Scarlet Letter.*

"You read a book? Voluntarily?"

"Of course I did." His hands gently caressed her back, applying light pressure to the sore spots right above her hipbones. "It's important to be educated."

She knew that. Hell, she had over a dozen pregnancy and baby books on her ereader. Read most of them more than once, too. But she was Practical Pru. Finn was...well, he wasn't a slouch when it came to education. He did have a BS in Fire Science and had to keep his EMT certificate up to date. She knew he studied hard for those. But she'd never known him to voluntarily seek education without an end goal. He didn't learn just to learn. He had to care about something to invest time in it.

He cares about you, dum-dum, and the babies.

She sucked in a sharp breath.

"What's wrong? Did I hurt you?"

Finn's concerned face came into view over her shoulder. She shook her head. "No. I'm fine."

He didn't press, but his wary gaze watched her for another moment before he returned to his massage.

Pru sat there with the knowledge she'd just discovered. Finn cared.

Duh, he was her best friend and the father of the babies, so of course he would care. But this felt different. He wasn't just offering to help or just tossing money at her for expenses. He was an active part of this journey. When she went to an appointment, Finn was there. Baby class, Finn was there.

Thinking back over the past months, she realized just how involved he was. He bought her preggy pops and pillows, read books to stay informed. Finn was going above and beyond anything they had discussed.

He cared. A lot.

What did that mean?

She could just ask him. It wasn't like they hadn't talked about almost everything under the sun during their years of friendship. So why was she holding back?

Because I'm afraid of what he'll say.

No. That wasn't it. Truthfully, she was afraid of the repercussions of what he might say and what it would mean. How that would change them. Their friendship had already changed so much recently. Pru didn't know if she could handle any more right now.

Besides, he hadn't changed his stance on subjecting a family to his risky job, and she hadn't changed her mind about solo motherhood. Even if Finn did want something more permanent, which she highly doubted, his occupation didn't match what she had in mind for a partner.

Like his occupation doesn't freak you out, anyway.

Pru wouldn't lie, her heart clutched with fear every time she heard a siren in the city, wondering if her best friend was responding, if he would be putting his life at risk to save others. She could only imagine how amplified that terror would be for the person who shared a life with him.

No matter what they were doing right now, he'd eventually want out. And that was fine with her. She didn't want anything permanent with him. She simply wanted her babies. So what if everyone here seemed to have a life partner who looked forward to spending year after year watching their children grow, sharing every birthday, holiday, and summer vacation. Relationships could wither and die. She knew that better than anyone.

Friendships are a form of relationship. Yours could die, too.

No. She and Finn were solid. They'd been each other's rock for years. Sure, they might have changed the dynamic of their friendship slightly over the past few months, but they could go back. She was sure Finn didn't have feelings for her. None other than friendship and a bit of lust.

Okay, a lot of lust.

And that's all she felt for him. Lust. Nothing more.

The instructor told the class to end the massage with a message for the baby. Finn's hand came around her to land on her belly, his head bent down, lips pressing to the slight roundness of her stomach as he spoke, just loudly enough for the words to travel to her ears.

"Hey there, babies. You grow big and strong in there because we can't wait to meet you. And you're getting the best mommy in the whole wide world, so try not to cause her too much pain when you make your big debut. She's a real wuss when it comes to pain."

"Hey," she complained, but he was right. She was a real, well, baby when it came to pain.

"But she loves you more than anything in this world, so don't worry. And I'll be there to help." He glanced up, mischief and caring filling the depths of his gaze. "She can squeeze my hand 'til it breaks if she has to. Whatever she needs, I'll be there."

Tears filled her eyes at his words. She had no idea what was going on, what she was feeling. This whole situation was becoming complicated, so much more than she'd ever anticipated. Or maybe it was just her pregnancy hormones going into overdrive. Yeah, that was it. She was seeing and feeling things that weren't really there. She didn't have deeper feelings for Finn, and he didn't have them for her.

It was all just baby brain.

And maybe a little sex haze.

Once these little bundles of joy made their appearance, everything would go back to normal. A new normal for her, to be sure, but she and Finn would go back to being just friends. Like they'd always been. Like it should be.

Nothing more.

Chapter Sixteen

F: *Picking you up in ten.*

P: *Make it five!*

Finn chuckled, reading the frustrated text from Pru on his cell screen.

F: *Bad day for a white wedding?*

P: *That joke was old the first seven hundred times you used it.*

So she said, but it still made the corner of her lips curl in the slightest grin. He'd stop telling it when she stopped secretly loving it.

F: *What's up?*

P: *Lilly and Mo are in uber-mother-hen mode today. They're stifling me.*

F: *They love you.*

P: *They're going to love me into uselessness if they don't stop freaking out over everything I do. I'm carrying babies, not the plague.*

He laughed because he knew Lilly and Moira were simply showing their care for Pru. No one wanted her overly stressed right now. In fact, Mo had texted, instructing him to play Pru classical music at night to calm her because stress wasn't good for the babies' emotional growth. He didn't even know fetuses had emotional growth.

F: *Ten minutes*

P: *FIVE!*

He smiled, slipping his cell into his pocket, checking on Bruiser, who lay happily in her doggy bed with her favorite chew toy, and headed out the door to his car to grab Pru before going over to his parents' place. He and Pru had been going over what to tell them about this whole situation. The past few family dinners she'd come to, it had been easy to hide her pregnancy, but now she was starting to show. And, besides, they'd find out eventually. He didn't like lying to his family, but the truth was…tricky.

Oddly, Pru had been exceedingly open to the idea of informing his mom and dad they were going to be grandparents again. She loved the idea of the babies having a big network of family to love and support them. As they discussed, she was still doing this mommy thing solo, but she'd agreed to let him help out. But even though she practically lived at his place now, they slept together almost every night, and he went to every checkup, he still got the impression Pru was holding back, like she was scared to admit what they were really doing.

Having a relationship.

He was smart enough to recognize it. And chickenshit enough to be terrified by it.

Somehow over the past few months, he and Pru had morphed from friends to lovers to relationship status. But what really scared him was that the anxiety-twisting knot in his gut, the one that always screamed "get out" whenever he was hanging with a date that might have serious potential, wasn't there. The only thing currently in his gut was a leftover burrito from lunch and a strange sense of comfort.

Could be the burrito. Could be Pru.

It probably wasn't the burrito.

So what did he do with this knowledge? He couldn't talk to Pru about it. They'd discussed a lot of hard stuff recently, but he knew Pru. If he let on for even one second that he was catching feelings, she'd run for the Rockies. He knew how Pru felt about the dangers of his job. Hell, it was the reason *he* didn't do relationships.

She needed a nine-to-five guy. A partner who would be home every night to help tuck the kids in, read them bedtime stories. He couldn't do that. He'd never imagined himself being that kind of person. But not being there for Pru and the twins...

He rubbed at the dull ache in his chest. The one that was getting stronger and stronger every time he thought too hard about the future. About what would happen once the babies arrived. He was afraid of what the growing ache signaled. Even though he knew he couldn't be the man Pru needed, a part of him longed to be the man she wanted.

He pulled up outside her apartment building, forgoing finding a visitor spot in the small crowded parking lot because there, standing just inside the glass front doors, stood Pru. The irritated expression on her face morphed into relief as she spotted him, then she threw open the front door and practically sprinted for the car.

"Careful," he admonished when she opened the door. "You're not supposed to run in your condition. You could fall and hurt yourself or the babies."

She slammed the car door, glaring at him. "Don't you start, too! Mo and Lilly haven't let me help all week. I've been stuck in the office while they went to the storage unit to grab all the boxes for the wedding we have next weekend."

He shrugged. "You're not supposed to be moving heavy boxes."

"They were filled with fake flowers and candles for centerpieces. I doubt any of them weighed more than five pounds."

"They don't want you to overexert yourself."

"They're acting like I can't do anything because I'm pregnant." She settled back into her seat with a pouty grunt. "I know they mean well, but they're driving me insane, and there's only so much work in the office to keep me busy."

Idle hands were not Pru's forte. The woman liked to stay busy. She also didn't appreciate people offering *her* helping hands. Not his Pru. Reaching over, he grasped her hand, bringing it to his lips for a soft kiss.

"They care about you. They're only trying to help."

"I don't need any help."

Yes, he was well aware of that fact. She repeated it to anyone and everyone who tried to lighten her load, as if offering help were some insidious trick people used, instead of an example of genuine caring.

"Yes, Pru. We all know you have everything under control and never need any help from anyone *ever*."

She pulled her hand from his, brow rising. "Wow, Finn, want a side of fries to go with that sarcasm?"

"You're the one acting like people caring about you is some insult." He shook his head. He knew Pru cherished her independence, but there was nothing weak about accepting help. He couldn't fight fires alone. He needed his crew to help him battle a natural force greater than he could ever be. "Letting the people who care about you help out isn't a bad thing. It doesn't mean we don't think you can do all this on your own—you're kick-ass, Pru, we know you are. We just want to support you."

He stared into those dark brown eyes, watching as the stubborn frustration melted away into reluctant acceptance. Her anger deflated.

"I know, but I'm starting to feel…"

"What?"

"Like I'm not pulling my own weight."

He snorted. The idea was ludicrous. As if Pru could ever give less than a hundred and ten percent in anything, especially her career.

"I guess I just didn't realize how much everything would change." She glanced down at her belly. "I mean, duh, I knew everything would change. But I wasn't prepared for how quickly it would happen. I just feel like everything is going so fast. I don't have time to catch up and assess the changes in the situation."

Only Pru would put it like that.

"Life is full of changes, Precious. They can happen in an instant or take years. Sometimes you just have to roll with it."

She arched one dark eyebrow. "When have I ever rolled with anything? And where did you get that crappy advice? The back of a beer bottle?"

"You rolled with me last night." He waggled his eyebrows. "Rolled right into reverse cowgirl—"

She smashed a hand over his mouth, laughter spilling from her lips. "Shut up and drive, perv."

Happy to see the smile back on her face, he did just that, taking them out of the city and into the suburbs. Once they arrived at his parents' place, he parked in the driveway.

"You sure you ready to do this?"

"Finn," she placed her hand protectively over her belly, "they're going to find out sooner or later. And since we decided you're going to be...helping out, I want the twins to know their grandparents. They deserve to have a loving family to build precious memories with. To learn things from. To go to when I'm being *the worst mom ever* to get hugs and candy."

He smiled, knowing the last one on her list was personal. Pru loved her great aunt, the older woman who'd raised her after her own parents had died. She'd been devastated when the woman passed. He knew she'd never deny her own children—his children—a chance to form that same loving bond she held so dear to her heart.

"Okay." He placed his own, large hand over her smaller ones, still amazed at what they'd created. "But you get to explain to them why you're not making an honest man out of their son."

"Oh, please." She laughed, opening the car door and slipping out. "Like your parents care about that."

She was right. Considering his parents had gotten married only after his eldest brother had turned one, he knew they wouldn't be surprised or upset by the less than traditional circumstances of their newest grandbabies.

He followed her out of the car to his parents' front door. She must have already knocked, because the second his foot hit the top step, the front door swung open.

"Pru, Finn, so glad you could both come tonight."

"Hi, Mom."

His mother reached out to hug Pru first since she was closer. After a moment in the hug, she pulled back, eyes wide. She glanced down to Pru's stomach, currently covered by her coat.

"Are you…?"

Pru nodded as his mother reached out to place both hands on Pru's stomach, rubbing over the fairly obvious bump there. Her gaze swiveled from Pru, to him, to Pru's stomach and back again.

"And it's…? You two…? You're…?"

His poor mother was going to suffer whiplash with all the back and forth.

"Congratulations, Mom." He smiled. "You're going to be a grandmother again."

Good thing no one in the house wore glasses, because the happy, high-pitched shriek coming from the woman who gave him life would have shattered them.

"Oh my! This is so exciting. I didn't even know you two were— But never mind about that. Come inside, we have to share the good news with everyone. Oh, I am so happy. You have to tell me when you're due. I have some of Finn's baby clothes if you want them."

He chuckled as his mother wrapped an arm around Pru's waist, one hand still on her belly, and ushered her inside, completely forgetting about her own offspring standing on the chilly porch.

"Come inside and close the door, Finn, before you let a draft in. We can't have Prudence getting sick right now."

Now he laughed, a full belly laugh, because of course his mother lover of all things baby—would focus all her attention on her newest grandbabies.

He followed the women inside, grabbing Pru's coat and hanging it with his own in the hall closet. Jordan had gone back to school, but his older brothers were there tonight with their families. The roaring noise in the living room quieted to a hushed din as he stepped in beside his mother and Pru.

"Everyone," his mother announced. "Prudence and Finn have some very exciting news to share with us."

Finn opened his mouth to speak, but his overly excited mother beat him to it.

"They're having a baby! I'm going to be a grandma again!"

Everyone stared in stunned silence for a beat or two before the room filled with boisterous noise. His brothers came over to pat him on the back while his sisters-in-law hugged Pru. His father—who sat in his chair, entertaining his current grandchildren with a storybook—lifted his head in congratulations.

Pru, having known his loud and excitable family for decades, still seemed a bit overwhelmed by the enthusiasm.

"Thanks, everyone." He maneuvered to Pru's side, resting a hand on her stomach. "But actually, Mom, we're not having *a* baby."

Everyone held their breath, happy smiles dropping slightly. He grinned. Wouldn't be family if he couldn't mess with them a little.

"We're having two. Twins."

The boisterous noise resumed. His mother smacked his shoulder with a scowl, admonishing him for scaring her. Everyone crowded around, asking questions, mostly about when Pru was due and how she was feeling. After a few minutes, the women went down to the basement to get some baby stuff his mother had been saving, and his brothers went into the kitchen to set up for dinner with the help of his nieces and nephews, all of whom had varying levels of curiosity about their new cousins.

Finn turned to go help set the table, when a motion from his father stopped him. Kurt Jamison was a man of few words. As a retired lawyer, words were his bread and butter, but he never minced them. He made each one count.

"You gonna marry that girl?"

See? Right to the matter at hand.

"Dad, first off, Pru is a woman, not a girl. Second, it's not 1950. And third, you didn't marry Mom until Quentin was one. I've seen the wedding album."

His old man shrugged. "True, but I proposed the day she told me she was pregnant."

Yeah, well, the day Pru told him she was carrying his baby knocked him onto his ass. They hadn't even been dating—not information his father needed to know—so marriage certainly hadn't entered his mind.

"Then why did you guys wait so long?"

Blue eyes, eyes the same color as his, stared back at him.

"Your mother said she didn't want me unless I wanted her. Your brother was an accident, but one she'd happily raise on her own if need be. She didn't want me proposing out of some silly notion of obligation then resenting the marriage *and* her years down the road."

Sounded like his mother. So why had his dad asked Finn about marrying Pru?

"The thing is, I loved your mother since the day I met her. Always have. I would have married her, baby or not. Took a while to convince her of that. To make her see I wasn't going to take off. I wasn't just sticking around because of the baby, but because of her. Because I loved her."

"Yeah, Dad, but Pru and I don't… It's not like… I don't love…"

At his nonsensical rambling, his father simply raised his brow.

"I'm not in love with Prudence."

Now his father laughed. *Not good.* Kurt Jamison only laughed when someone told a witty joke or a cat got scared by a cucumber. His dad emailed him so many of those stupid videos. He seriously regretted showing the man how YouTube worked.

"What?"

"Son, you've been in love with that girl—woman—since the tenth grade."

Had not.

"You may be able to hide it from everyone else, including your mother, which is a feat of God in itself, but you can't fool me. I know." A warm hand landed on Finn's shoulder. "I've been there. The Jamison men tend to fall for tough, stubborn women. Stay strong, son. Don't let her push you away, because I know she has feelings for you, too."

"How do you know?" *Dammit*, he hadn't meant to ask that. He hadn't meant to admit his father might be right.

Might. Because, yeah, he could admit to himself—and only to himself right now—he had been harboring a secret crush on Pru for a long time, but a crush didn't equal love. He cared for her. Deeply. In a more-than-a-friend kind of way that some people might call love. Y'know, if you believed in all that sappy stuff.

His father smiled, placing both hands on Finn's shoulders and staring him straight in the eyes. "Don't let her push you away. Prove yourself and your feelings and don't let doubt or fear overwhelm you. Either of you."

Great. He'd just do…that. Simple, right?

"Dinner's ready," Quentin called from the kitchen.

The women arrived back upstairs a moment later, all of them surrounding Pru, still offering advice and tips on pregnancy and babies. Her arms were empty, but his mother carried a box overflowing with baby blankets, clothes, and a toy puppy he'd remembered sleeping with every night until he was in the fifth grade.

"Here, Finn, dear." His mother dumped the surprisingly heavy box into his arms. "Put this in your car so you two don't forget it, then join us at the table."

"Sure, Mom."

He rolled his eyes, catching Pru's gaze. She laughed,

shrugging as his mother pulled her into the kitchen. She looked good here, happy, surrounded by his family. A place she'd always been welcomed, a place she'd now be a part of forever. A place he suddenly realized he never wanted to be at without her.

Dammit.

Why were parents always right?

Chapter Seventeen

"I've got cheesecake!" Mo raised the dessert high in the air as she entered the apartment.

Pru grinned from her position on the couch. "Perfect. I just cued up the movie, and once Lilly's out of the bathroom, we can start girls' night."

Her roommate set the delicious confection on the coffee table before taking a seat next to Pru. Small but surprisingly strong arms wrapped around her shoulders and tugged her in for a hug.

"Ugh, it feels like forever since we've had a girls' night. I can't believe we let it go this long."

Some of that was Pru's fault. Okay, most of it. Though the women lived and worked together, they tried to set aside one night every few weeks to just kick back and relax, not as business partners but the way they began—as friends. Since they were in their downtime as far as weddings went, it should have been easier for them all to find a night off, but she'd been spending more and more time at Finn's place.

She hadn't meant to neglect her other friends. She just

had a lot going on right now.

And now she sounded selfish and awful.

Guilt filled the empty portion of her stomach she'd been saving for the sweet cheesecake, and Pru winced. "I'm sorry I haven't been around much after work." At least she was still paying her share of the rent and bills.

"Oh please," Mo chuckled. "If I could share a bed with a hot, sexy fireman, I would, too."

She nudged her friend. "I can arrange that. Want me to tell Ward to text you?"

The blond woman snorted. "No way. Ward is a fine piece of eye candy no doubt, but he and Díaz are meant for each other, and I am not one to stand in the way of true love."

Really? Díaz and Ward? Pru figured the two would kill each other before they kissed each other, but far be it from her to correct Mo, the eternal optimist.

"Anyone make popcorn yet?" Lilly asked, coming into the room.

"I did." Pru held up the large bowl of buttery popcorn, handing it over to her roommate and snagging the small bowl she'd put aside for herself.

"What's that?" Mo raised one pale blond eyebrow.

"Popcorn."

Mo peeked into the bowl, rearing back with a horrified shudder. "No. That is not popcorn. That's a culinary crime."

She glanced at the contents of the bowl in her lap. "It's not that bad."

Lilly leaned over the back of the couch warily to eye the ingredients of Pru's pregnancy popcorn mix.

"Is that…gravy and hot sauce?" One perfectly manicured hand came up to cover her mouth as she gagged.

"Not hot sauce." Mo wrinkled her nose. "Smells more like strawberry sauce."

"Oh, Pru, sweetie. That's disgusting." Lilly's bright green

eyes grew wide. "You're not actually going to eat that, are you?"

"Back off, you two." She clutched her bowl tighter to her chest just in case her taste-impaired friends tried to nab it from her and dump it down the disposal. "Yes, it's mushroom gravy and strawberry syrup over popcorn, and yes I'm going to eat it. It's got carbs, veggies, fruit. Everything the babies need to grow big and strong."

Mo scooted to the other end of the couch. "You've had some weird cravings, honey, but this tops them all. Even I wouldn't try that."

And they all knew Mo would try anything.

"Can we just sit and watch the movie, please? My doctor says it's fine to eat whatever I crave as long as it's not on my forbidden food list."

"That should be on the list."

She ignored Mo's comment and Lilly's nod of agreement. So maybe this was one of her stranger pregnancy cravings, but—*mmmmmmmm*—she moaned as she lifted a few fluffy kernels drenched in savory, sweet goo to her lips, relishing the odd mix of flavors exploding on her tongue.

"What?" she mumbled around her mouthful at the horrified expressions on her friends' faces. "It's delicious."

Mo shook her head, blond curls, highlighted with streaks of purple this week, tumbling around her shoulders. "Pregnancy is weird."

True. Had she not been craving this particular concoction of tastes, she would one hundred percent agree that what she was currently putting in her mouth was disgusting. But the babies wanted what they wanted, and she was already a pushover for those tiny little ones who held such a big part of her heart. So here she was, eating mushroom gravy popcorn topped with strawberry sauce and loving every bite.

Mo and Lilly stayed on the far side of the couch for

the first half of the movie. The very far side. But once her delicious—thank you very much—treat was done, both women scooted over. They finished the movie and popcorn and made a sizable dent in the cheesecake. Since Finn had just started his twenty-four-hour shift, Pru decided to crash at home tonight. She'd checked on Bruiser before coming back to her apartment and planned on going back to Finn's in the morning to feed the sweet girl and take her to the park for some much-needed exercise.

Maybe it was her burgeoning mommy instincts, but she'd been spoiling the pup with too many dog treats, and the little Yorkie mix had gained a bit of weight.

"That movie was hilarious." Mo stood, grabbing the empty popcorn bowls and heading to the kitchen. "Hollywood needs to make more female buddy movies. I laughed so hard I almost peed."

Lilly grimaced. "I'm glad you didn't, considering I was sitting next to you. But you're right, it was very funny."

Pru concurred. Then again, anything with Kate McKinnon could make her laugh. That woman had a direct line to her funny bone.

Grabbing the empty water glasses, she started to rise from the couch, but the second she did, a sharp, stabbing pain hit her right in the side of her lower abdomen.

"Ouch!"

"Sweetie?"

"Pru, honey?"

Immediately her friends were there, one on each side, holding her arms, gently lowering her back to the soft cushions of the couch. Mo grabbed the glasses from her hands, placing them on the coffee table while Lilly crouched in front of her, green eyes filled with concern.

"Pru, what is it? What hurts?"

"My side." She placed a hand to her right side, fear

seizing her lungs as she tried to pull in a deep breath. Why couldn't she breathe? It wasn't her chest that hurt, it was her side. What was going on?

"You're hyperventilating, sweetie. Now look in my eyes and breathe deep with me." Lilly squeezed her hand. "In and out. That's good. Again, in and out. Good. One more time, in and out."

There. There was the oxygen she needed.

Now that she could breathe again, she could focus on the real problem. The sharp, pulling pain just above her hipbone.

"The babies." The words fell from her lips without thought. She had no idea what was going on, but based on the vicinity of the pain, all she could think of was the twins. She'd just entered her second trimester—the first held the most risk of loss, but she knew that didn't guarantee anything. A million more things could go wrong.

Her side pinched again. What was happening? Every pregnancy book and health pamphlet she'd read fell right out of her brain. She couldn't think, couldn't reason, couldn't imagine what was going on, only that she was in pain. Her heart seized with fear that something was wrong with her babies. "Lilly…"

"It's all right, Pru. We'll call the doctor. I'm sure nothing is wrong with the babies."

"Yeah." Mo tried to give her a teasing smile, but it fell flat. "I'm sure it's just indigestion from that monstrosity of a snack you inhaled."

She knew her friends were trying to keep her spirits up, but right now nothing would make her feel better. Nothing except the all clear from her doctor. Unfortunately—

"The office is closed," Pru said.

"Then we'll go to urgent care," Lilly replied. "Just a few blocks away. Mo, go pull the car up front."

Mo hurried out the door, for once readily doing Lilly's

bidding. Pru took a deep breath, grateful Lilly was so good in a crisis and that they lived in the city, where the nearest all-night healthcare facility was less than ten minutes away. Right now, every second she sat there in pain, not knowing what was happening, felt like an eternity.

"Why don't you call Finn?"

"I can't. He's at the station. His shift just started. He can't leave."

"Prudence." Lilly leveled her with a hard stare. "Call him."

Her hand slid to her phone, thumbprint unlocking the cell and hitting Finn's number without her brain even being conscious of doing it. The phone rang and rang, each peel of the tone ratcheting her already frazzled nerves higher and higher.

Where was he? Why wasn't he answering his phone?

She sucked in a deep breath, trying to push down the bile that threatened to rise in her throat due to the fear currently racing through every inch of her.

"Hey, this is Finn. Sorry I can't take your call, but you know what to do."

A shrill beep filled her ear, and it took Pru a moment to realize the machine had started to record. She took a deep breath, trying her best to keep the panic and fear out of her voice.

"Finn—" She choked back a sob, gathering herself. She could handle this. There was no reason to fall apart. Not until she knew for certain something was wrong. Right now she had to remain calm. Be strong for the babies.

Her hand rubbed her stomach, willing all the health and love she had in her directly into those two tiny lives inside.

"Finn," she started again, voice strong this time. "I'm having some slight pain, so Lilly and Mo are taking me to urgent care on Eighth. Just, um…wanted to let you know."

She hung up, clutching her phone tightly in her grip.

"He didn't answer." She glanced up to Lilly, fear once again causing her voice to tremble. "Probably on a call or something."

Lilly helped her stand and gently led her to the door, face filled with sympathy and concern.

"Oh, sweetie, I'm sure he'll call you as soon as he can. Finn cares about you and the babies, but his job—"

"His job is important." She knew that. He had a very important, very dangerous job that would always come before any other obligation in his life. Like kids or a relationship. She didn't need to be reminded of it.

But, apparently, she did, because for the past few weeks, they'd been playing house, pretending everything was fine and they could carry on with this situation that looked remarkably like a real relationship. The forever kind.

But things weren't fine. Something was wrong. She needed Finn and he wasn't here for her. That wasn't entirely fair of her to think, but her mind was so consumed with fear for the twins, all rationality had flown away. The only thing she knew was that she was scared, she needed Finn, and he wasn't here for her.

. . .

Finn had never driven faster in his life, not even in the fire truck with sirens blaring. The moment he got Pru's voicemail, his heart shot up into his throat.

Finn, I'm having some slight pain.

Pain. Pru was in pain. Where was the pain? How bad was it? Was she okay? Were the babies okay? The fear in her voice came through clear as a bell in her message, even though he knew she'd tried to hide it. Dammit! If he ever found the punk that pulled that prank fire alarm they'd been called to, he would make the kid scrub the rig for a solid month with nothing but a toothbrush.

Luckily, the station wasn't too far away from the urgent care, and the chief had given him the all-clear to take off. No one pulled him over. Even if they had, he would have explained the situation and gotten a police escort. He knew a lot of men and women on the force, having worked with them from time to time. Cops and firefighters might have a rivalry on the baseball field for the annual charity game, but off pitch, they both worked to keep the city safe. They needed each other. And right now, he needed to get to Pru.

He'd never heard distress like that in her voice before. Not even when her aunt Rose took a turn for the worse and they knew the end was coming. Pru was always so strong, so fearless. Truth be told, his gut had jumped up into his throat the moment she uttered his name in a broken whisper on the message. It hadn't settled since.

He never dreamed of being a father. It hadn't been his plan to have kids, ever. But when Pru told him she was pregnant, something sparked to life inside of him. No. That's wasn't it. Something in him had always sparked when it came to Pru, he'd just been damned good at shoving it way deep down into the darkest corner of his soul. But it was becoming harder and harder to deny the truth.

He loved Pru.

It was time to stop hiding the way he felt. They were friends, lovers, and they were having babies *together*. Time for him to man up and have a good sit down with her. A heart to heart. He knew she had to feel…something for him. Pru didn't sleep with people on a whim. There had to be some secret feelings she'd buried like he had. Otherwise none of this would have happened. Right?

First things first.

He had to get to the doctor and make sure the woman

he loved and the unborn babies who already held his heart in the palms of their tiny hands were all okay. Everything else he could deal with later.

He pulled into the urgent care parking lot, racing inside to find Mo and Lilly pacing the waiting room floor. But no Pru.

"Where is she?"

The two women stopped their frantic movement, both staring at him in shock.

"Finn?" Lilly raised her brow, pushing her glasses back up her nose when they slipped down.

He cut her off. "I got Pru's message. I was on a call, but as soon as I could, I raced over here and—"

"It's okay, Finn." Mo came over to his side, giving him a strong hug for such a small woman. "She's back in the exam room now. Can he go back?" She angled her head to the side, speaking to the woman at the front desk. "He's the father."

The woman nodded, smiling softly at him. "Room Four. Just straight on back and on your right, sir."

With a slight nod, he gave Lilly and Mo an appreciative smile, or as much of a smile as he could muster with all this fear and adrenaline rushing through his veins. Pulling away from Mo, he turned and rushed down the hallway, stopping in front of the light brown door with the number four on it. He needed to take a moment and breathe. Pru needed him to be calm, in control. He had to be strong for her. He couldn't rush in there all high-strung and freaked out. It wouldn't be good for her or the babies.

He ran a hand over the top of his head, fingers tangling in his hair, tugging on his scalp, trying to use the slight sting to center himself. After a deep breath where his heart went from a hundred to a mere ninety miles an hour, he decided it was the best he could do. With a quick knock and the turn of the knob, he entered the room to find the woman he loved sitting on the exam room table wearing nothing but a cloth gown and a worried expression.

"Pru." His heart slowed at the sight of her. Rushing to her side, he cupped her face in his hands, a small measure of relief filling him at seeing her sitting up. That had to be good, right? Nothing could be too terribly wrong if she was sitting up, right?

"Finn?" She shook her head, her soft cheeks rubbing against the roughness of his palms. "What are you doing here?"

Where the hell else would he be?

"I got your message. I'm sorry I didn't answer my phone. We were on a call. Is everything okay? What did the doctor say?"

"They haven't been in yet."

So many emotions passed over her face—worry, panic, confusion, anger—each one piercing his heart like tiny stabs from a hot poker.

"I'm sure everything will be fine." He pulled her into his arms, trying to give her the reassurance she needed even if he knew nothing of the sort. "You're going to be okay, the babies will be okay. I'm here for you, Pru. I love you."

She stiffened in his arms. "You what?"

Shit.

Had he really said that? Out loud?

Yeah, he had. Dumb move. Now was not the time to tell Pru how he felt, but his brain was so scattered. Going from fear to relief back to fear all in the space of a few minutes kind of killed his mind-to-mouth filter.

"Finn, what the hell do you mean you—"

A soft knock on the door interrupted her. Finn stepped back, releasing her from the circle of his arms, but grabbing on to her hand. He knew he'd chosen the wrong moment to declare his feelings, but right now he needed the physical connection to her. Evidently, she needed it, too, because instead of wrenching her hand away, she held tight, squeezing as the doctor appeared.

"Ms. Carlson?"

Jim Gibbs, a doctor Finn had worked with before on a few emergency calls, stepped into the room.

"Dr. Gibbs."

"Finn. I wasn't aware this was a fire department emergency."

"It's not. Pru is my...she's...we're..." Shit! What did he call her? His girlfriend? His friend? His lover? None of those terms fit.

"Oh. I see."

Thank God the doc did, because Finn couldn't see anything beyond his blind panic.

"So, Ms. Carlson, I understand you are fifteen weeks pregnant with twins and experiencing some abdominal pain?"

"Yes."

She squeezed his hand so tight he feared loss of circulation. Didn't matter. He'd cut the damned thing off if it would help her in any way.

The doctor glanced at the chart in his hands. "Any bleeding? Excessive vomiting? Heart palpitations? Severe back pain?"

She shook her head. "No. My morning sickness disappeared about two weeks ago, and other than a little stiffness at the end of the day, my back is fine."

"Okay, I believe I know what the issue is, but why don't we have a look, just to make sure?" Dr. Gibbs grabbed the small, portable ultrasound machine from the corner of the room.

"Yes, please."

Pru kept a tight grip on his hand as she lay back on the

exam table, lifting her gown to expose her bare, round belly. He stood by her side, stroking her hair with his free hand, kissing her temple, whispering encouraging words he didn't feel.

"Ah yes, this looks good." Dr. Gibbs smiled at them. "See, baby one and baby two."

He pointed to the screen, where Finn could see the two blobs had formed into almost human-like shapes. Holy crap!

"Healthy heartbeats, healthy sizes. Everything looks just fine, Ms. Carlson."

The doctor pushed the machine away and handed Finn a tissue, which he used to gently wipe the goo off Pru's belly.

"So what is this pain I'm experiencing?"

"Round ligament pain. Very common in pregnant women, especially with twins, when the muscles and skin stretch more rapidly." The doctor made a note on his chart. "Nothing to worry about, but if the pain gets intense or you experience any bleeding, please come back right away or call your OB-GYN. But right now I see no need to worry. Your babies look healthy and happy in there. Keep up the good work, Mom and Dad."

"Thank you, Doctor," Pru said with a relieved sigh.

Finn sent the man a grateful smile. "Thanks, Gibbs."

Dr. Gibbs nodded, leaving them alone in the room.

Pru sat up with a sound halfway between a sob and a laugh. "Oh my God. I feel so relieved and like such a dummy all at the same time."

"You're not a dummy." He cupped her face in his hands. "You're a good mom. Already you're worrying about the kids' health."

"Yeah, imagine the freak-out I'm going to have when they get their first cold."

He laughed along with her, leaning in to kiss her lips softly. "You're going to be great, and don't worry, I'll be there to curb any mommy freak-outs you have."

The terror and stress of the past half hour fell away, common sense leaving his body along with all the anxiety, and he opened his mouth and uttered the last words he ever should have spoken at that moment.

"I think we should move in together."

Chapter Eighteen

Could a person get emotional whiplash? Because Pru was pretty sure she was suffering from it at that very moment.

I love you, Pru. I think we should move in together.

She didn't even know what to do with those statements. A sob escaped her lips right before a torrent of warm, wet tears started to pour down her cheeks.

Burst into tears, apparently.

"Oh shit." He grimaced. "Don't cry, Precious. Please. I didn't mean to make you cry."

But he had. Because on top of the stress of worrying about the twins, now she had to deal with her best friend thinking he was in love with her when she knew he wasn't. They had a good system going. Why was he ruining it?

"Y-y-y-you don't l-l-love me," she stuttered between sobs.

One dark blond brow rose. "I *don't*? Then why did I say it?"

"Finn." She pinched the bridge of her nose, trying to figure out a way to reason with an unreasonable person. She took a few deep breaths to get her emotions under control before she spoke again. He didn't love her. The very idea was... She didn't know exactly what it was. Not possible.

Once her breathing had gone back to normal and her tears had dried, she used the corner of her gown to wipe up her face. Straightening her back, she stared Finn directly in the eye. One of them had to be logical in this situation. "We just suffered a big scare. Your emotions are all over the place right now. You're not thinking clearly."

"I'm thinking clear enough to know you're full of bullshit."

"Excuse me?"

He ran a hand over his head, a common move she knew he did when frustrated. *Join the party, buddy.*

"I know the past half hour was scary—hell, Pru, the past few months have been terrifying."

"Terrifying?" Sure, finding out she was pregnant by Finn, with twins, had been a bit of a shock, but she'd planned to become a mom. She wasn't scared by it.

"I don't mean the babies," he said, reading her mind. "I mean us."

"Us?" Great, now she was so confused she'd been reduced to repetitive one-word questions.

"Our relationship."

"Finn, we don't have a relationship." Friendship, yes. Bedship, hell yeah. But an actual long-term, committed, this-is-going-somewhere relationship? No.

"Really? You've practically moved into my place already. We sleep together almost every night, neither of us is dating anyone else, and we're having kids together. If that's not a relationship, then what the hell is it?"

The frustration poured off him in waves. The long vein at the base of his neck, right below his ear, started to pulse in the way it did whenever he got angry. Which wasn't often, but it tended to happen when he had to deal with drunk driver accidents. She'd seen Finn mad before, but the emotion had never been directed at her. He seemed plenty upset with her right now, though. And this was so not a conversation she wanted to have with her pants across the room.

Slipping off the exam table, she crossed to the small chair in the corner where she'd set her clothes. She grabbed the leggings, shoving first one leg then the other into the soft, stretchy material, grateful she still had her underwear on. Being naked during a fight made her feel at a disadvantage.

She knew Mo would tell her to use her nakedness to end the fight and win, and if it were any other argument, she might consider it. But this wasn't a small argument about not doing the dishes or eating the last piece of pizza in the fridge. This felt big. An uneasy calm before an impending storm that would rip away everything she held dear. She had to stop this.

"Finn, you've never had a long-term relationship."

"What do you call us?"

"I meant a romantic one." Friendships didn't count. "Look, we've only been sleeping together for a few months, and we both know it's just a fling."

He arched a brow. "We do?"

Stuffing her head into her oversize sweater, she righted the garment before turning. "That's what we agreed to."

"No."

He stalked toward her, lifting a hand and cupping her face in a gentle move, contrary to the tense emotions vibrating off him. "We agreed to be together until the itch was satisfied, and I don't think that's ever going to happen, Precious. Why do you think I've never managed to hold onto a woman for long and you've dumped every loser you've gone out with?"

"Hey! Not every guy I've dated has been a loser." And technically Terrence dumped *her*. But it wasn't like she went chasing after him, so what did that say about her true feelings for her jerk ex?

He pressed closer. "Really? Then why aren't you still with any of them?"

She tried to come up with an answer, but it was difficult to think when he was standing so close. She could feel the heat of his body pressed up against hers. Lately, her breasts were so sensitive, all it took was a glance from Finn to get her raring to go. So weird. Here they were, having an argument in an urgent care exam room after a scare that knocked ten years off her life, and she was turned on.

Baby hormones.

She was going to blame it on the baby hormones. But that excuse could only stretch so far, and it sounded weaker and weaker each time she used it.

"Wanna know what I think?"

Not really, since she suspected it might be too close to the truth and she really couldn't handle that right now. But Prudence Carlson had never been a coward, so she raised her chin and stared directly into those stubborn, beautiful eyes.

The left side of his mouth curled up at her bravado.

"I think the reason I don't make it past a first date, and you check every single man you've dated against an impossible list of standards, isn't because my job is too dangerous for a family, or because you need that perfect nine-to-five, white picket fence fantasy. It's because we both know no one is right for us."

She sucked in a harsh breath at his bleak and accurate words.

"Because we're perfect for each other."

Say what now?

His right hand still cupped her face, the left coming up to grasp her hip in a protective hold.

"We've been best friends forever, but there's always been a spark of attraction. Don't deny it."

"I'm not denying the physical attraction between us."

They'd been sleeping together for months, and she still got turned on any time he so much as smiled at her. It'd be pretty stupid of her to deny the spark. Didn't mean they were in love with each other. Lust did not equal love.

"I think that neither of us has taken the chance to see if we could be something more because we've both been too scared. Scared of losing what we had, losing our friendship if we took it to the next level and it didn't work out. But it did work, Pru. It *is* working. And it's not a temporary thing or some silly itch I feel for you. I love you." He pressed his forehead against hers. "I know my job can be terrifying, but life is terrifying. There are no guarantees for anyone. I can't keep using it as an excuse not to go after what I want, who I want. And I want you, Pru. And the babies. Maybe the timing was never right, or we had to grow up a little, but we crossed that line, and I don't want to go back."

Sure, he said that now, but what about a few months down the road when they had two screaming babies at home needing feedings and diaper changes and constant care? She'd planned for it, but Finn hadn't. He would miss his single life. The freedom of it.

He'd never abandon her. She knew that, because he was a good person and never backed down on a commitment. But she didn't want to be his commitment. She didn't want to risk him staying then resenting her for the situation he found himself in.

"You don't want this."

The hand on her hip tensed. "Don't tell me what I want. I want you. I want to wake up by your side and fall asleep with you in my arms." He kissed the tip of her nose. "I want to see your lists and charts spread all over the kitchen table and argue with you about whether our favorite holiday drink is pronounced wass-*ale* or wass-*el*."

The small laugh that left her lips sounded suspiciously

like a sob. "It's wass-*ale*."

"Wass-*el*." He grinned, tipping his head to brush a soft kiss against her lips. "I want to wake up to screaming babies at two in the morning and change smelly diapers and worry about how we're going to afford the kids' college when we still have our own student loan debt. I want it all, Pru. Because when you love someone you don't just want the fun times. You want everything. The good and the bad."

She wanted to believe him, so badly. But he'd sprung this on her, and she didn't know what she was feeling, what she was thinking. Sure, she'd admit to some starry-eyed fantasies lately about the possibility of something more, but she had no idea if they were something she really wanted or just a symptom of pregnancy. This was all so complicated.

"Finn, I…"

He pulled her into him, hands going around her back. She wrapped her arms around him, taking strength from his hug even as her mind screamed in terror at the decision she had to make. Take a chance on love and possibly lose her best friend, or try to push things back to the way they were and always wonder what could have been?

"This is ridiculous. We shouldn't make important decisions during such an emotional time."

His body tensed against hers. A small whimper escaped as he pulled away, his warmth and comfort leaving her feeling cold, worried. Pale blue eyes, filled with pain and sadness, stared at her.

His jaw clenched as he shook his head. "You can't ration out feelings, Pru. It doesn't work like that." He ran a hand over his head, blowing out a frustrated breath. "I think the real problem here is that you're afraid."

Duh! She was going to be a mom. Every new parent was afraid. It was written in the parent handbook.

"You're afraid of love."

What? All she wanted in life was someone to love. It was the exact reason she'd started this journey into motherhood in the first place. She shook her head, denying his words and the tiny spark of fearful truth they ignited deep in her soul.

He ignored her protest and pushed on. "You take care of everyone—your roommates, me, Bruiser. You give all your heart and love to everyone, but you are so damn afraid to take any love for yourself. And I don't get it." He took a step, cupping her face in his hands, staring deeply into her eyes. "You, more than anyone I know, are so deserving of love, Prudence. But you're also so afraid to take it when it's offered. And I can't force you to take mine. Even if I rip my damn heart out and offer it to you."

With a sad sigh that pierced her chest like a physical blow, he dropped his hands and turned toward the door.

"Finn?"

He paused, his back to her. She cleared her throat, trying to keep her wobbly voice steady as tears gathered in her eyes. She wanted to crest this mountain of fear. To tell him she loved him, to forget all her anxiety and rationality and agree to spend the rest of her life loving him, but she didn't know how. How did one overcome a lifetime of loss and insecurity? How did people allow themselves to be loved?

"Are…are we…?"

His head turned, face glancing at her over his shoulder. A hopeful light brightening his eyes.

"You're still my friend, right?"

The hopeful light died, the brilliant blue fading to a dark, miserable gray.

"I promised to be your friend, and I will. No matter what happens. You have my friendship forever." He turned away from her again, the soft, defeated words leaving his lips as he opened the door. "But I…I can't do *us* anymore, Pru. Not when you won't admit what we really are. It hurts too damn much."

Pru sucked in a sharp breath at his words as he headed out of the room. She felt like all the air had been pulled from her lungs. Pain that had nothing to do with any physical ailment assaulted her. She could feel Finn's misery as surely as if it were her own. And maybe it was. She was such an emotional mess right now that she didn't know what to think.

Knowing the urgent care was busy and they'd already stayed too long in the exam room, Pru waited thirty seconds then followed Finn out. Thankfully, he was gone by the time she entered the waiting area. Lilly and Mo sat in the small room, speaking in hushed whispers. At her arrival, they both immediately rose and rushed to her side.

"Sweetie, is everything okay?" Lilly asked, eyes full of concern.

Mo's hand went to her stomach. "Are the babies—"

"The babies are fine." She tried to dredge up a smile for her friends but found she had none. "Everything is fine."

Lilly used one finger to push her glasses up her nose. "Really? Then why did Finn just walk out of here like a kid who's been told Santa doesn't exist?"

Something warm and wet rolled down her cheeks. Mo grabbed a tissue from her purse, dabbing at Pru's eyes.

"Oh, honey. What is it?"

"Finn loves me."

Her roommates glanced at her as if she were growing two heads instead of two babies.

Lilly patted her hand. "Of course he does."

"You knew?"

Mo snorted. "Everyone knows. Anyone who's spent more than two minutes in your presence can see that man is head over heels for you. Always has been."

What the hell?

"B-b-but he goes on so many dates!"

Mo snorted. "Denial ain't just a river in Egypt."

"Come on." Lilly wrapped an arm around her shoulders, leading her toward the front doors. "I feel like this is a discussion better had at home."

But they didn't finish the conversation at home. Because Pru went directly to her room and stayed there the entire night, curled up on her bed, rubbing her stomach and second-guessing every word she'd uttered in that exam room.

. . .

Over the next few days, she went over what Finn said to her about a million times in her head. What had he meant by they were still friends but not an "us"? She wanted to ask him to clarify, but he hadn't called or texted. She hadn't heard one word from him since he left the urgent care.

She hadn't tried to contact him, either. She'd thought about it a dozen times every hour, even composed a few texts, but she didn't have the guts to send them. For the first time in all their years of friendship, he wanted something from her she didn't think she could give him. Every time she imagined what it would be like to share her life fully with Finn, fear reached up and choked her.

On Thursday, three days after the urgent care visit, she came home from putting flowers on her parents' and Aunt Rose's graves, a visit she made monthly. But this time she felt different as she stared at the dark gray slabs etched with the names and dates of the people she'd loved and lost.

Losing them had torn a hole in her, shaped her entire life, but so had their love. Did the pain of their loss negate the years of love she still held in her heart for them? Was Finn right? Was she just letting the fear of loss cloud her mind to what she truly felt deep in her heart?

All this emotional upheaval was exhausting.

She needed a nap.

Unfortunately, the moment she stepped into her apartment, she saw Lilly and Mo standing in the living room, staring at her, their body language tense. Her nap would have to wait.

"Hey, guys." She shifted nervously at the serious expression on both of her roommates' faces. "What's going on?"

"What's going on," Mo said, "is an intervention."

Lilly sighed. "It's not an intervention, Moira. It's a conversation."

"This is a safe space," Mo continued dramatically, opening her arms, a wobbly smile on her face. "We're concerned about you."

"She's right on that point," Lilly agreed.

Pru tried to smile, but it fell flat. "I'm fine."

Her friends shared a look. Mo came over to her, gently grabbing her arm and leading her to the sofa, where the three women sat.

"You're not fine. You've been mopey all week."

"I have not been mopey!" Sad, confused, scared? Yes. But not mopey.

"Just tell us what's wrong, sweetie." Lilly patted her hand.

The storm of emotions she'd been holding inside for the past few days broke like a dam. Her friends' concern tore down that last bit of resistance she'd been holding onto. Releasing a deep breath, she told them everything Finn had said to her that night at urgent care.

"Sounds about right," Lilly stated, when she finished.

"Yup," Mo agreed.

What? They could not be serious!

"Are you two kidding? You think Finn and I have been in love with each other for years but have been too scared to do anything about it?"

Mo held up her hands in surrender. "I didn't say it. You did."

She'd done no such thing.

Okay, she had, but only because they inferred it.

"Sweetie," Lilly grasped her hand. "Isn't it possible that the measuring stick you hold other men to is impossible to achieve because deep down you're judging them against Finn and no man can measure up to him?"

"Finn's not perfect. He has flaws."

Lilly nodded. "Tons of them, I'm sure."

He did. He was a cover hog. He always threw his damp towels on the floor instead of hanging them up. He liked coconut milk. What perfect person liked coconut milk?

"We're not saying he's perfect," Mo grabbed her other hand. "We're saying he's perfect for you. You two fit together. You're soulmates. Perfect matches. Happily-ever-afters. He's your one, Pru and you're his."

"But his job," she protested.

"It's dangerous," Lilly nodded in agreement. "But no one is promised tomorrow."

"Yeah." Mo patted her hand. "I read about some guy who choked on a hot dog and died just last week so unless you plan on consuming all your food in liquid form, you could die just as easily as Finn."

Lilly gasped, "Moira!"

"What? All I'm saying is death can happen to anyone at any time and using a dude's job as an excuse not to go for true love is only something only a dummy would do." Pale brown eyes stared at her. "And Pru is no dummy, right?"

Of course she wasn't a dummy. She was terrified. Terrified of admitting what she truly felt because opening herself up like that meant opening herself up to the possibility of loss and pain. She'd already had so much loss in her life. Could she risk more?

Risk aversion. Playing it safe. Practical. Practical Pru.

Oh no.

Drawing strength from the two intuitive women holding her together right now, she gasped. It was pointless to deny the truth any longer. Silent or screamed, it still existed, and pretending it didn't wouldn't change the fact.

"Oh my God! I love Finn!"

"There ya go," Mo grinned. "Sometimes ya have to hit them over the head with it."

"But...I..." Her head swiveled from one friend to the other. "What do I do? What if we do this and things don't work out?"

Lilly smiled, pushing her glasses up her nose as they slipped down. "You have to decide if you're willing to take a risk that things might work out and whether you can accept any fallout if they don't. Life doesn't give us a guarantee. Not in anything."

"Isn't a chance at happiness, a chance at true love, worth it?"

Mo had stars in her eyes, but for the first time in all their years of friendship, Pru wanted to believe in those stars, too. She wanted to take the risk, leave her charts and lists behind, and see if that tiny spark deep inside her heart would grow into something bigger if she recognized it and let it out.

"I—" Two strong pops of gas flopped in her belly. Only they weren't gas. They were... *Oh my God!* They were kicks! "Oh!"

Pulling her hands away, she placed both on her belly and waited.

"Pru, what are you—"

"Shhhh!"

She shushed Mo, waiting, silent, hoping...there! It happened. A small kick followed by another. Her babies. They were in there. Growing, healthy, filling her heart with so much love she could barely contain it. Tears ran a warm path down her cheek, but this time they were happy tears. She loved her babies, and she loved their father. Had for years, probably, but she'd been too stubborn to see it. Too scared.

She wasn't afraid anymore.

Liar.

Okay, she was terrified, but love was more powerful than fear. She knew there were risks, life was a big ol' ball of risk, but what kind of life would she have if she never went for what she truly wanted? What kind of example would she set for her babies if she didn't try to gain her heart's desire? They were her first step toward finding her true happiness, and their father was now her second.

But she'd hurt her best friend.

Badly.

She hadn't believed in them, in him. And he said they couldn't be an "us" anymore. Had she ruined her chances with Finn, or would he be willing to give her a second chance?

She would have to grovel, prove his words got through to her and that she could conquer her fear, allowing them to be together. And she had to do it in a way that he knew she was serious.

"Mo..." She turned to her roommate, a huge grin widening her lips. "Get me some paper. I need to write up a plan."

"I'd go for the running dramatically to his side and declaring my love in the pouring rain, but since it's not raining and it's you, I'd say a precise plan is the perfect way to go."

As Mo hopped up to grab the requested paper, Lilly handed her a pen from the coffee table with a knowing smile. "I think we're going to need some cheesecake."

The only thing Pru needed was Finn, but a plan and a little more cheesecake couldn't hurt.

Chapter Nineteen

Finn finished his fifth set of pushups, collapsing and rolling over to his back. Maybe he'd overdone it on the workout, but he needed to blow off all this dark energy clouding him. He'd returned to the firehouse after leaving Pru at urgent care in the capable hands of her roommates. Then he'd cut short his days off and picked up an extra shift for one of the crew who came down with the flu, because what the hell else was he supposed to do? Go home and sit there, worrying he'd made a giant-ass mistake by pushing the woman he loved into something she wasn't ready for?

Unless she doesn't love me.

The terrifying thought sank into his psyche, making his bleak mood even darker. It was entirely possible that Pru didn't feel the way he did. To her, this whole thing might just be a case of long suppressed lust. Just because he felt something deeper, didn't mean she did.

No. He didn't believe that. Pru wouldn't have slept with him if she didn't feel something. Even the tiniest bit of caring. Maybe it hadn't started out as love, but it sure had grown into it. He knew it. How could they not love each other? They were best friends, dynamite in bed, loved hanging out with each other. Were they perfect? Hell no. No relationship was perfect, but they respected each other, trusted each other, and worked out their issues together.

Wasn't that love?

He had no idea. All he knew was ever since he told Pru how he felt and witnessed sheer panic fill her eyes, he'd begun to have doubts. Not about his feelings. He loved Pru. Nothing could ever convince him he didn't. He knew his heart, and right now, the thought of not being with her had it splintering, a physical ache spreading out into every inch of his body, weighing him down with the gloom of what his life would be like without her in it.

He knew what he wanted. Unfortunately, there was no way for him to know what Pru wanted. Not until she figured it out for herself and shared it with him.

If that ever came. It had been days since they'd talked or even texted. He couldn't remember the last time they'd gone this long without contact. He felt like he was missing a limb.

Or his heart.

"Hey, *dude-bro*." Díaz tossed Finn a bottle of water. "Might want to take a break from working out before you snap a muscle."

He snatched the bottle out of the air, twisting off the cap and gulping down the entire thing. The cool liquid did nothing to quench his thirst for an answer, but it did solve his dehydration problem. His fellow firefighter was right. He needed to cool it on the fitness. He'd be no use to his crew or the people who needed their help if he got a muscle tear from over exercising. Time to find a new distraction.

"Thanks." He tossed the empty bottle into the recycling bin. "I'm going to hit the shower then make dinner."

"It's Ward's night to cook."

Sure, but cooking would occupy his hands and brain so he didn't think about Pru, worry about Pru, miss Pru.

"Do we want dinner or food poisoning?"

"Hey!" Ward yelled from outside the workout area. Popping his head in the small room, the man scowled. "I'm not that bad of a cook, and I'm making spaghetti tonight. Not even I can mess up pasta."

He begged to differ. Last time Ward made pasta, it was so al dente Finn damn near chipped a tooth. The man was a badass firefighter, but he couldn't cook worth shit.

"Just because Pru is taking her pregnancy hormones out on you, doesn't mean you get to be a pissy dick to the rest of us."

It wasn't pregnancy hormones. Hell, he wished it were. This went deeper. When you denied something long enough, it took on its own life. Could become real. Maybe the years they'd spent ignoring their true feelings for one another wiped them out? It hadn't for Finn, but perhaps it had for Pru. Maybe it wasn't time she needed, or fear she had to face. Maybe she simply didn't love him.

And wasn't that a shitty truth to swallow.

So, yeah, maybe he was being a *pissy dick* as Ward so eloquently put it, but he had good reason. The woman he loved might not love him back. That was enough to turn any person into a raincloud.

"I'm hitting the shower."

He pushed past his friends and crewmates, heading to the tiny showers with shitty water pressure that barely trickled enough to wash the soap off his back. While vigorously scrubbing off all the sweat and negative thoughts of the past few hours, he tried to look at the bright side of things. Tried to stay positive.

What if she never comes around?

The thought burned through him hotter than any fire

he'd ever fought. But he had to admit, even if only to himself, it was a real possibility. Pru might never love him, And what would he do then? Work out until every muscle in his body died of exhaustion?

Whatever he did, he'd still be by her side. Still be her friend. He'd promised. And there were the twins to think about. No way would he abandon his kids. Pru might want to take the lead, but he'd damn sure be there every step of the way, helping as much as she'd let him.

Shutting off the poor excuse for a shower, he dried off and tugged on a fresh pair of pants and a Denver Fire Department T-shirt.

The loud high-pitched yip of Bruiser echoed through the vent in the bathroom.

"Bru Baby?"

He knew all his dog's barks. The hungry bark, the squirrel bark, the "evil delivery man is at the front door and I'm your big, bad guard dog" bark.

But this one...this one he recognized as her "happy to see her second favorite human" bark.

Pru?

His heart raced in his chest, beating faster than it had over the past few hours of torture he'd put it through with his vigorous workout. He hurried out of the bathroom to the main area, where he saw his crew sitting around the table, lovin' on his pup and talking to the woman who held his entire heart in her hands.

The second he stepped into the room, her gaze swung up as if she'd felt his presence. That had to be good, right? But her worried expression made his gut sink.

"Pru." He hurried to her side, his hand automatically reaching out to cover her stomach. "What's wrong? Is everything okay with the babies?"

Maybe the doctor ran more tests after he left, or called

with news, or maybe she'd had more pain. Shit! He shouldn't have left her. Sure, she had her friends and she'd told him to go, but he should have insisted on staying and taking care of her.

"I'm fine, the babies are fine. But, um, I was wondering if we could talk?"

The last time she asked that, it turned his entire world upside down. He wasn't sure if he could handle another spin.

"Yeah, sure."

Grasping her hand, he tugged her into the workout room, away from prying ears, though he knew his crew was listening because they were all a bunch of gossips.

"What's up?'

She took a deep breath before launching in. "So, I know you're still on shift until tomorrow morning, but we have a wedding this weekend, and I wanted to do this before that."

"Do what?"

Digging through her purse she came up with a folded sheet of paper. One of her very detailed lists, no doubt. A smile tugged at the corner of his lips. His Practical Pru. God, he loved her so damn much.

"Here."

She handed it over. He took it, making sure to brush his fingers along hers as he grasped the piece of paper. He felt her tremble at the contact, hoping it was a good sign, but when he glanced at the slip, his brow drew down in confusion.

"What's this?" He stared at the black ink, what appeared to be a list of addresses with prices next to them, written in Pru's familiar handwriting.

"It's a list of potential apartments we can afford." She pressed on when he didn't comment further. "You said you wanted to live together."

Yeah. He also said he loved her, which was something people usually declared before they took the next step in a relationship.

He knew what Pru was trying to do—at least, he hoped he did—but he wasn't letting her off easy. No. She had to fully admit what she felt if they were really going to do this thing.

Folding the list, he handed it back to her. She stared at the paper, refusing to take it, and left it hanging, suspended in his fingers in the air between them.

"You don't like those places?" She tugged on her ponytail. "It wasn't my most thorough research. I can find more places if you want. I was just trying to find locations close to the firehouse and—"

"It's not about the location, Pru," he interrupted. "Why?"

She shook her head. "Why what?"

Okay, looked like they were doing this the hard way. He held the paper up a bit higher. "Why did you make this list? Why do you suddenly want to live together?"

"Because you offered."

He shook his head.

She scowled. "Because we're having twins together, and you want to be involved."

He took a step toward her. "Try again, Precious."

Frustration pulling at her lips, she threw her hand up in the air. "Because I love you, you big, stupid jerk!"

Relief washed over him. He closed his eyes, savoring those words and the warmth they filled him with. A smile tugged up the corner of his lips. He opened his eyes and speared her with a teasing look. "Big, stupid jerk?"

She ripped the paper from his hand, lightly smacking it against his chest. "I was trying to apologize and prove to you that I love you by coming up with a plan for our future."

He chuckled. "Without actually apologizing?"

Her eyes narrowed.

Pulling her into his arms, he laughed out loud. "I'm sorry. Did I ruin your grand plans?"

Crumpling up the paper, she tossed it over her shoulder, wrapping her arms around his waist.

"Yes, you did." She sighed, pulling back. "But it's probably for the best. Lately my plans have been getting waylaid left and right, and the more I think about it, the happier I am, because as much as I try to plan out this perfect life, it's not going to happen. Life is messy and complicated and unpredictable. I can try as hard as I want to steer it where I want it to go"—she rubbed a hand over her baby bump—"but it's always going to surprise me with how things turn out. And I know some of those surprises will be bad, but some will be happy and…scary."

"I scare you?"

She huffed out a small laugh. "You terrify me, Finn. You're the only person who has seen me at my best and my worst. You're the one I run to first when I have good news, bad news, any news. You're the one I never get sick of spending time with and who always accepts that anything I'm feeling is okay. I can be myself around you one hundred percent of the time."

"And that's scary?"

"Yes!" Her teeth came out to worry her bottom lip. "Because it means losing you would be like losing a part of myself. You were right, Finn."

His lips curved up into a full-blown grin. "I'm right? Bet that hurt to say."

She smiled along with him. "Shut up, ass."

"Ooooo, such sweet love names you give me."

The teasing light left her eyes, replaced with something warmer, something deeper.

"I do love you, Finn. I'm in love with you, and I have been for a while now. I was just too afraid to admit it. I do want to live with you, raise our babies with you, build a life with you. I want to let you in, full partnership, to help with whatever I need." Her nose scrunched up as she finished her statement. "Even if I'm too stubborn to ask for it."

Weight dropped off his shoulders. The tension he'd been carrying melted away. Not only did she love him, but she just gave him a blanket acceptance for all future help. He smiled to himself, knowing he might need to remind the fiercely independent woman he loved that she'd agreed he could be her support system, something he knew was hard for her to admit needing and a task he was humbled and honored to accept.

He took a step, reaching out, hauling her into his arms as his mouth came crashing down on hers. Pru's hands came up to wrap around the back of his neck. Her mouth opened, tongue swiping against his bottom lip, seeking entrance. Far be it from him to deny her anything. He opened for her, greedily drinking in the rich, heady taste unique to Pru. This kiss was unlike any they'd ever shared. There was a promise in this one. A future. A recognition of love.

His entire body sighed in relief with the knowledge that this was the first of many. He'd taken a risk by revealing his true feelings. Best risk of his life, turned out.

"Hey, Pru?" he whispered against her lips.

"Yeah?"

Her sweet eyes stared up at him, a dreamy, content expression filling their dark brown depths. Made him feel ten feet tall to know he was the one who put it there, he was the one who she felt safe enough with to finally let down all her walls and admit the truth of what she felt. What they both felt. Still, it was them, and he wasn't letting her get out of this whole situation without poking a bit of fun.

What kind of best friend would he be if he didn't tease her just a little?

"Can I get it in writing that I was right? I feel like I'm going to need it when you're cursing my name and blaming me for 'doing this to you' in the delivery room."

"Be more of a cliché, Finn."

She rolled her eyes, but the smile on her lips grew wider. Bending his head again, he pressed a kiss to that spot on her neck that always caused her to make an adorable sexy squeak.

Yeah, he was a goner. Hook, line, and sinker. For the rest of his life he would do anything for this woman. Anything to make her laugh, smile, moan, and, yes, even squeak.

"Oh good, it looks like they made up," Ward's voice carried into the small room from the doorway. "Now maybe Finn can stop being such a grumpy SOB."

Finn continued to focus on Pru, lifting one hand to flip off his fellow firefighter. He heard a soft chuckle before the sound of footsteps carried the man away and left him alone again with the person who mattered most to him in this world.

"Were you being pouty, Finn?" Pru chuckled as if it was the funniest thing she'd ever heard.

"Watch it, or I won't give you your surprise later."

She snorted, staring down at his crotch. "Yeah, pretty sure I'll get my *surprise* no matter what I do."

He placed a hand to his chest, mouth dropping open in faux shock. "Are you implying that I'm easy?"

"For me? Damn right."

She had him there. For her, he'd do just about anything. But the little minx was wrong about one thing. Her surprise wasn't sex—okay, that would probably be an added bonus— but for the real treat he planned, he'd talked to his buddy who was a chef at one of Denver's most popular diners and gotten his famous recipe for chili cheese fries. He figured if he couldn't win her back with the power of his love, maybe he'd win her over with food. Worth a shot. And now it'd be worth brownie points.

He should make her brownies, too.

His mind buzzed with all the ways he planned on

pampering and spoiling Pru. She deserved it. Not only was she one of the most amazing people he'd ever known, she'd given him the greatest gift he could have ever received. Her love.

"Oh!" Her face lit up. She pulled back, the smile stretching her lips until her entire expression reflected pure joy. Reaching out, she grabbed his hand and placed it on her round belly. Confused, Finn obliged, resting his palm on her stomach until—

Holy shit!

Something hit his hand. Like the flex of a stomach muscle, only in one tiny concentrated spot. Not a flex, but a kick. A tiny baby kick. His baby and—there it went again! Another one, or the other baby. He wasn't sure, but suddenly it became hard to breathe, his eyes watering with the immense and awe-inspiring implication of what he'd just felt.

"Was that…?"

"Yeah," she nodded, her own eyes welling with tears. "They're saying hi to their daddy."

Daddy. He was going to be a daddy with his best friend, the woman he loved, the person who made him feel complete and all that other cliché crap he'd never believed in until one night he made the best worst decision of his life and slept with Pru.

He rubbed her stomach, trying his best to say "hi" back to the two little souls he couldn't believe he loved so much already. With his free hand, he cupped Pru's cheek, dipping his head to press a soft, but very thorough, kiss to her lips.

"I love you, Prudence Carlson. Thank you so much for loving me back."

"Well, it was the least I could do, since you gave me my heart's wish."

He glanced down. "The babies?"

She shook her head. "No, but thank you for them, too.

You gave me love, Finn Jamison. Free and clear and so unconditional there was no way I could deny my own love for you. I always knew I wanted to be a mom, but I never knew I wanted to be an 'us' until you."

"Glad I could be so helpful." He kissed her once more before pulling back and nodding toward the door. "Now let's go pretend to eat some of Ward's hard-as-rock pasta and when I get off shift, I'll take you home and make you anything you want."

She grinned, eyes heating. "How about a delicious Finn and Pru sandwich?"

Damn, he loved this woman. "Whatever you want."

And he meant it. He would do whatever he could to make Pru happy because without her, he couldn't be whole.

Chapter Twenty

"Okay, Ms. Carlson, your stitches look good. How's your pain level?"

Pru smiled at Doctor Richardson. "It's manageable."

Anything from here on out would be manageable after fifteen hours of labor followed by an emergency C-section. Poor Simon was breech and blocking in his sister Sasha. As hard as she and the doctor tried, they couldn't get the sweet little baby boy to turn. Finally, they'd decided to go in and get the babies, for the health and safety of everyone. Not quite the birth plan she had mapped out, but as life so beautifully taught her this past year, things often failed to go according to plan.

She couldn't complain. Just look what her failed plans got her. Two perfect, adorable, healthy babies, a wonderful, sexy partner who would do anything to make her smile—and did, everyday—and as a bonus, she was now a proud pup mommy, too.

During month six of her pregnancy, when they realized she was practically living full-time at Finn's, she did a much more thorough rental search than her initial "win Finn back" list. After clearing it with Lilly and Mo—who'd given her a farewell party complete with plenty of tears, cheesecake, and a suspicious lack of gravy or jelly-related foods—she and Finn found a surprisingly affordable two-bedroom townhouse in the Cap Hill area of Denver. They planned on buying a house soon, but with the babies arriving, they didn't want to add that stress to their plate. For now, they had the much-needed space and, bonus, a yard for Bruiser to run her little doggie legs off.

"Good. I'm going to approve you for solid foods now, so feel free to place an order with the hospital kitchen, and they'll send something up right away. But try to keep it light. Nothing too spicy for the time being."

Yes, food! She hadn't eaten anything since she'd arrived at the hospital last night. She was starving. And thirsty. Ice chips were a joke, and she hated their stupid, frozen uselessness.

"Thank you, doctor."

Doctor Richardson smiled. "Congratulations again, Mommy." With that, she turned and left the room.

The moment the doctor was gone, Pru reached for the binder on her bedside table containing all the hospital's pertinent information, including the cafeteria menu. She winced as the movement caused the stitches in her abdomen to pull slightly.

Gentle movements.

She'd have to remember that for the next few weeks. Geesh, whoever said C-sections were the easy way out obviously never had one.

She flipped through the book until she found the page she was looking for. Everything sounded delicious. Her stomach grumbled with hunger, or maybe it was her organs shifting back into place after releasing two six-pound babies. Didn't matter. She could eat solid foods, hallelujah!

After deciding on a turkey sandwich with a fruit bowl and chocolate chip cookies, she called in her order. The kind-sounding woman on the other end of the phone promised it would be up in the next fifteen minutes. Her mouth watered in anticipation. Had she ever been this hungry before? If so, she couldn't remember.

"Knock, knock?"

She glanced up to the doorway to see two familiar and very welcome faces.

"Lilly, Mo! It's so good to see you both."

The women rushed inside, Lilly placing a vase with a lovely arrangement of flowers on her bedside table before reaching down to gently hug her. Mo, with two adorable stuffed puppies in her arms, her hair streaked with orange this month, glanced around the room.

"Where are the babies?"

"The nurse came to take them for their first bath. Finn went with."

"Such a sweet daddy." Mo placed the stuffed animals next to the flowers and nudged Lilly out of the way to get her own hug.

"So…" Lilly moved to her other side, placing a hand on her shoulder. "How are you feeling? Finn kept us updated on everything. An emergency c-section? That sounds scary."

It had been, but everyone had pulled through okay, thanks to the wonderful hospital staff. And Finn, of course, who was by her side every pain-filled, terror-inducing second. He'd been her rock, just like always. How she ever could have denied loving that man was beyond her.

"Yeah, it was, but we're all okay, and that's the important thing."

"I can't believe you're awake." Mo shook her head. "Aren't you tired?"

Exhausted, but she'd gotten a few hours of sleep in the recovery area, and honestly, she was still riding the high of seeing her sweet children's faces. *Children*. She was a mommy. Her dream had come true and so much more because she got Finn along with it. Who knew her heart desired more?

"We're back, Mommy."

Pru tilted her head to see around Mo, a smile curving her lips as Finn and the nurse came in, wheeling two baby bassinets in front of them.

"How'd they do?" She tried to get a look at her babies, but from the angle of her bed, it was hard to see down into the bassinets.

"Sasha is a little fish." Finn grinned, looking down at his daughter. "She loves the water. Simon, on the other hand, cried the entire time."

"Oh no."

"Don't worry," the nurse said with a kind smile. "I think he was just grumpy because his sister got to go first. You two are going to have your hands full with these sweet little bundles."

"They'll be fine." Mo winked. "They've got help."

They did have help—from her amazing friends and Finn's awesome family. It filled her heart to bursting to know that so many people already loved her babies. They had a village surrounding them to love and care for them. A family of blood *and* heart.

The nurse smiled, leaving them alone. Pru lifted her arms.

"Gimme." It'd only been about half an hour, but she already missed her babies. Man, she was going to smother these kiddos with love. They'd be sick of her by Tuesday.

"Hold on."

Finn glanced at Mo and Lilly, the three of them sharing some strange unspoken conversation. Her friends smiled, stepping away from her side as they moved to the far end of the bed. Mo pulled her phone out of her pocket, trying to be discreet about it, but Pru saw the woman hold it up, camera facing Pru.

What in the world was going on?

"Finn?"

"The babies have a present for their mommy."

She laughed. "They're less than a day old and they already have a present for me? I think I'm going to like being a mom."

He said nothing, simply smiled, lifting the nearest baby into the cradle of his arms and carefully walking the few steps to the bed where she lay. When he placed the baby in her arms, she glanced down, immediately knowing she was holding Sasha. How? Call it a mother's instinct or the distinct forehead freckle she'd noticed on her daughter right after they'd pulled her out and held the precious baby up for mommy to see.

The white blanket with tiny footprints her daughter had been wrapped in before her bath was gone, replaced by a white playsuit that had the words *our daddy?* printed on it.

"Huh?"

They'd gotten a lot of silly baby clothes with jokes varying from dumb to hilarious over the past few months, but this one she didn't get.

Finn leaned over her, his smiled turning into a frown as he read the garment.

"Shit! I mean, shoot. Sorry, babies. Daddy didn't mean to say a bad word."

He was freaking adorable. "Pretty sure they can't understand curse words yet, babe."

He pointed a finger at her, gently grabbing Sasha from her arms and placing a soft kiss to her lips in the process. He turned, placing their baby in her bassinet, and then reached over to grab Simon. Bringing the tiny boy to her with the same care he used with his sister, Finn grinned.

"There. Simon was supposed to go first, but much like with the bath, I guess Sasha is always going to be one step ahead of our boy."

Growing up an only child, Pru had no experience with sibling rivalry. Good thing Finn had experience in spades.

She glanced down to see that Simon had something written on his clothing as well. Words that, when paired with his sister's, made Pru's heart stop.

Will you marry

A choked sob sounded in the room, and it took a minute for Pru to realize it came from her. Suddenly another small weight filled her arms as Finn set Sasha next to Simon. The sweet twins nuzzled each other, grasping hands as they settled together as they had in her womb. Sasha gave a small yawn while Simon softly snored, and all Pru could do was read the message on their clothing over and over again.

Will you marry our daddy?

The writing became blurry as tears filled her eyes, and she glanced up to see Finn's smiling face, a slight hint of panic and worry behind his gaze. Oh please, like she'd ever say anything but—

"Yes!"

"Wahoo!"

The shout came from Mo, she thought. She didn't know, because the moment she uttered the acceptance, Finn leaned in to take her lips. A slightly awkward kiss, what with two sleeping babies between them and her in a hospital bed, but it was the most amazing kiss of her life. It signified a new beginning, a continuation, a confirmation that life moved of its own will regardless of her plans, and that was okay. She was coming to find she very much liked her plans getting mixed up.

"I love you, Pru," he whispered against her lips.

"I love you, too."

"Oh my God!" Mo stopped filming and jumped up and down. "I just realized we get to plan your wedding. This is so exciting!"

"We can certainly get you both a very good deal. Every vendor we know will do it for cost, I'm sure." Lilly nodded.

She didn't care about weddings or costs or any of that stuff at the moment. The only things that mattered to her were here in this room. She'd gladly get married right now if there was a justice of the peace available. Sacrilege for a wedding planner to say? Maybe, but she knew it wasn't the day that was important, but the life you built around it.

So sure, they might have a big fancy wedding or a small intimate one. Honestly, whatever Finn wanted was fine with her because she had her friends, her babies, and the man she loved. What more did she need?

"Hello?" A tall, skinny kid who looked no older than eighteen popped his head into the room, a large tray covered with a silver dome in his hand. "I have an order for Prudence Carlson?"

Food. She needed food.

"That's me."

The kid placed the tray on the rolling table, moving it over to her bed. Lilly and Mo jumped at the opportunity to snatch up the twins, each woman cuddling and cooing to the babies as they both sat in the chairs opposite Pru's bed.

"What? No chili cheese fries?" Finn smirked as Pru lifted the lid off her dinner.

"You can make me a whole plate of them later." Somehow the man had learned to make killer chili cheese fries, a new talent she was incredibly thankful for.

He leaned down to kiss her softly. "I'll make you whatever

you want when we all go home."

Home.

So funny how less than a year ago that word meant something different. Now it was so much more. Not just a place she rested her head or kept all her stuff. She had her home with her friends, the office and their old apartment where she knew she'd be participating in girls' nights at least once a month—as Finn insisted—and she had her home with Finn and now the twins. Not the house they rented, but the place in their hearts where their love for each other lived.

Because no matter where life took them, no matter what messes their plans turned into, she knew they would always be there for each other, just like they always had been. Family was what you made it, and she'd made hers with Finn. It wasn't what she set out to do, but she was so very glad it happened. And she couldn't wait to see what new twists and turns life threw their way.

She glanced down at the sad-looking turkey sandwich and questionable fruit dish. At least the cookies appeared edible. One touch, and she realized they were harder than a rock. She'd probably chip a tooth if she took one bite.

Didn't matter. Food was food right now. Finn grabbed the cookie from her fingertips, bringing the dessert to her lips. She smiled, taking a bite that wasn't as bad as she feared. He stroked her cheek, a wealth of love in his eyes. Love for her. It still floored her, every time she saw it.

She knew, right then, no matter what happened in the future, they could handle it. As long as they were always by each other's side, they could handle anything.

Even hospital food.

Acknowledgments

I'd like to thank Dalton and Tessa for letting me ask a million questions about what life as a firefighter is like and what it's like to love one. I'd also like to thank Sam for taking me through the crazy journey that is the life of a wedding planner. Any mistakes made portraying these professions are mine alone.

A huge thanks to my agent Eva Scalzo and my editors Stacy Abrams and Judi Lauren for believing in me and working so hard on this book with me to make Pru and Finn's story the best it could be. Also a big thank you to all the staff at Entangled Publishing for all their support and dedication on this book.

Lastly I'd like to thank my wonderful family for all their love and support especially my Prince Charming who is always there with a cup of coffee, strong martini, or comforting hug. Whatever I need, you always provide. Thanks babe!

About the Author

Bestselling author Mariah Ankenman lives in the beautiful Rocky Mountains with her two rambunctious daughters and loving husband who provides ample inspiration for her heart-stopping heroes. Her books have been nominated for the prestigious RWA Golden Heart® and CRW Stiletto awards.

Whether she's writing hometown heroes or sexy supernaturals, Mariah loves to lose herself in a world of words. Her favorite thing about writing is when she can make someone's day a little brighter with one of her books.

Find love in unexpected places with these satisfying Lovestruck reads...

THE BEST FRIEND INCIDENT
a *Driven to Love* novel by Melia Alexander

Stacey Winters's best friend Grant offers her a window into the male psyche—and sets the bar high for her future Mr. Right. But then she accidentally crosses the friend zone and kisses him. Grant Phillips doesn't do relationships. "No attachments" is his hard and fast rule. There's only one exception: his best friend, Stacey. But now that he knows how good it felt to kiss her, felt the addictive slide of her body against his, Stacey Winters is indelibly stamped onto Grant's brain—and not just as his friend.

HER SUPER-SECRET REBOUND BOYFRIEND
a novel by Kerri Carpenter

It wasn't shy librarian Lola McBride's idea to crash someone else's high school reunion. Her best friend made her do it, insisting that having fun with a super-hot rebound would make her forget about her breakup. That's when she meets the hottest guy she's ever seen. Architect Luke Erickson catches the sexy brunette in a lie, and counters with a proposal. From one reunion to another, Lola and Luke are suddenly spending a lot of time together. Good thing they're only pretending, or this super-secret relationship could get really complicated.

Made in the USA
Lexington, KY
08 November 2019